Distracting the Heir

WENDY MAY ANDREWS

Sparrow Ink
www.sparrowink.com

ISBN - 978-1-989634-55-4

www.wendymayandrews.com

Stay in touch with Wendy May Andrews
and forthcoming publishing news.

Sign up for her biweekly newsletter

Distraction is a luxury he's never been able to afford. Until now...

Constance Moreland can't fathom anything more *boring* than traditional marriage. So, she's perfectly happy living a wealthy spinster's life, traveling and having adventures. But when her paid companion longs for home, Connie agrees to attend a society house party with her. She assumed those in attendance would be of little interest. Then *he* arrived and she realized just how wrong she'd been...

Florent Alcott is long overdue for some adventure. Years of struggling to right his family's fortune and provide for his siblings have left him feeling older than his actual age. So, he readily accepts an invitation to his neighbor's party, hoping for something *exciting* to happen. He just never expected that *excitement* to come in the form of the lovely and endlessly fascinating Connie...

But when an unexpected enemy arrives, can an impractical lady and an ever-practical gentleman thwart the villain in time to claim their happily ever after? Or will their time together be nothing but a pleasant—and fleeting—distraction?

Distracting the Heir is a sweet and clean standalone Regency romance with perfect chemistry, memorable characters, a hint of intrigue, and a satisfying happy ending.

Dedication

Constance is determined to be an eccentric even if that moniker doesn't fit so very well. This book is dedicated to both the independent souls as well as the conventional ones. There is room enough for everyone

XO

Acknowledgements

Acknowledgment number one has to go to my best friend and life partner, Mr. Andrews. Thank you for putting up with the late nights and takeout while I whittled away at this story. Thank you too for knowing and caring about my Northcotts nearly as much as I do. You're the best walking and talking partner a gal could ask for. Thanks for helping get in both my steps and my words.

Acknowledgment number two must go to my parents. Thank you for always standing by me and supporting me in all my endeavors. Thank you for loving my books and cheering me on. Thanks too for reading to me as a small child. I blame you for my love of words.

My beta readers – Alfred, Monique, Suzanne, and Christina – thank you so much for cheering for me, finding the plot holes, and making such fabulous suggestions to help the stories improve.

My gorgeous cover is thanks to the artistry of *Envision Literary Photography* and Les at *GermanCreative*. I'm thrilled with my beautiful covers in this series.

My editing team, Bev Rosenbaum and Julie Sherwood, are experts in their field. I am grateful for their input. The characters' goals and motivations have certainly deepened with their help as well as ironing out the kinks in this story and timeline, and putting in all the commas that I always leave lying about. Any remaining mistakes are entirely the fault of the author.

Chapter One

Lady Constance Moreland, last daughter and youngest child of Viscount Moore, was getting a little tired of being an original. It had seemed like such a good idea when she had come up with it but, she thought with a sigh that she quickly turned into a light cough followed by a serene smile, it was turning out to be far duller than she had anticipated.

Take this house party, for example, Connie thought as she glanced around the well-appointed room in which she and her fellow guests were gathered. She really ought to have remained on the continent where she was praised and feted for having thoughts in her head other than the latest fashions and tidbits of gossip. But here, rather than anyone other than her hostess thinking she was brilliant, most of the other ladies avoided her studiously while the gentlemen seemed determined to prove that a lady who has chosen to remain unwed was of questionable moral fortitude. Perhaps it was because she wasn't sitting at home doing needlework but had instead chosen a more adventurous life, but Connie couldn't understand how or why that would bring her judgment or morals into question.

Connie struggled to make friends. It was a challenge to avoid eye contact with gentlemen staring at her admiringly while also trying to appear open for conversation if the conversant was another woman. She was never sure she had pulled it off. She supposed that was why she heard whispers that she was standoffish. Connie was relieved that she had at least her paid companion at her side. But even poor Peggy wanted to be rid of her, just for different reasons than the others. Peggy was the most devoted of friends but Connie knew she wanted a different life than they were currently living.

The social situation Lady Constance faced was truly tiresome. Perhaps she ought to just go home. But that would be admitting defeat. And a Moreland would never admit such a preposterous thing. Besides, Grandmother Asquith, the darling old curmudgeon who had inspired her and made her life of travel possible, would never forgive her if she were to find out Connie had been so insipid. Of course, the fact that Grandmother had died would make that challenging, but still, it was the principle of the matter. Constance had to stay the course. Even if she at times wondered why she had thought it was such a brilliant idea in the first place.

Take her hostess, Lady Adelaide, for example. She clearly had a brain in her pretty head. And her husband evidently adored her and supported her "fits and starts" as he sometimes called his wife's original ideas. And yet, if Constance wasn't mistaken, the viscountess was with child. As an aging maiden, Constance was well aware that many would be scandalized that she was even aware that was a possibility, but she had grown up in the country with lots of animals about. She had a rudimentary idea of where babies came from. And with her older sisters already married and starting their families, it was impossible not to know at least a little bit, even if she was supposed to keep that knowledge to herself.

It was the most ridiculous thing and one of the reasons she should have stayed away. At least on the continent some of these ridiculous, staid ideas were kept under bounds. Connie wanted to ask her hostess about her pregnancy but conventions held her back. It made Constance feel rude. Surely the viscountess would be excited or possibly nervous about the future arrival. Wouldn't she *want* to talk about it?

Of course, Lady Adelaide had friends and family that she was far closer to than her guest. In fact, Constance wondered what prompted her being invited at all. She had discussed the matter extensively with her companion, Peggy. Or rather Miss Smith. Connie had to keep reminding herself that they were back in polite society and she had to mind the conventions. She couldn't refer to her companion in the familiar while in company. Since that was terribly hard for Connie to remember, she had taken to trying to refer to her companion, even in her mind, as the more formal Miss Smith rather than how she had taken to call her for the past two years.

Speaking of, Connie thought with a smile as she glanced around the room. Where had her companion gotten to? Shouldn't she be, well, keeping her company? That was her assigned role for goodness' sake.

Not that Connie ever really needed company. She found her own company to be the most stimulating. Having a companion was merely one other convention she had to abide by. And it was the only way her family could countenance her travels. And Peggy, Miss Smith, was the only person both she and her family could agree upon. She was suitably acceptable to chaperone Lady Constance Moreland but not too dull to bore Connie to tears.

And they were related besides. Distantly, but still, family is family, Connie thought. It must be the worst sort of uncomfortable being the poor relation. While being a paid companion had to still be difficult at times, Connie had done her best not to make the other woman feel awkward in her company.

But the poor dear had been pining for home, which was why Connie had accepted this invitation. Well, that and the fact that she had been a little bit homesick herself. But she should have known that home wouldn't be homey for her anymore. Constance was beginning to suspect that she would never be comfortable anywhere.

Once you stepped out of the box Society had assigned you, you couldn't comfortably settle yourself back into it again. But also, no other box was home. It was quite the conundrum. Connie suspected soldiers probably felt the same way only probably far worse since they had done and witnessed things that they could never talk about.

She had, of course, done and witnessed things she could never talk about, too, but it was a far different matter. She couldn't describe the crispness of the air on that mountain in Italy to someone who had only ever spent time in London or on their estate. How could she describe the deep blue of the lake she had come across on the top of that same mountain to someone who hadn't seen something similar?

No, being an original was a rather lonely existence. And having a paid companion didn't make it any less lonely.

Constance's eyes swept the room again. Miss Alcott was missing as well. Was it possible the girl was with Peggy, Miss Smith? Not terribly likely. *Where was she?* Miss Alcott was the most interesting woman Connie had yet met on this recent foray back into polite society. Constance would like to further the acquaintance, but the other young woman kept disappearing. Connie had started to think the girl might be pursuing some of the other activities house parties had a reputation for. She hadn't thought Miss Alcott seemed the type nor that Lady Adelaide would countenance such a thing, but how else to explain the woman's frequent absences? Then again, Peggy was often absent, too, so perhaps there were other things going on. She would have to investigate. The thought filled her with anticipation.

Her eyes narrowed in thought which she quickly adjusted. It wouldn't do to appear calculating as one lady had already accused her of. Connie stifled another sigh. She should have known better than to accept Lady Adelaide's invitation, but it had been so very tempting. Here she was, though, only one day into her stay and already wishing to leave. She supposed she could fabricate an emergency of some sort, but that would require that someone write to her, which was an unlikely event.

No, she would have to make the best of it and try to see the humour in the situation. It would just be easier with the seeming protection of her companion by her side. If only she had the ability to make friends easily like some ladies seemed to possess. No, Connie had to pay for a companion. And said companion couldn't even be relied upon to stay by her side.

Finally, Constance took herself to task. Perhaps the poor dear was sick or some such. She ought to go check on her rather than sit here thinking poorly of the other woman. Just because she was paying her didn't mean Miss Smith was actually her servant. And while her employment ought to give her a sense of obligation toward Constance, Peggy wasn't actually expected to be at her beck and call every waking moment. Still, it unsettled Constance to feel so alone in the assembled crowd, so with a serene smile pinned to her face, she glided from the room.

"Oh, my apologies," a deep voice said as Constance nearly collided with a large man. A shiver danced down her spine as he briefly clasped her arm to prevent her from stumbling. A delicious one. An unfamiliar sensation, to be sure. He quickly removed his hand from her person but it felt as though he left an imprint even though he hadn't hurt her in any way.

"No harm was done," Constance replied as she quickly stepped away from him, ignoring the inexplicable urge to remain exactly where she was. She tried, too, to ignore the breathy quality of her voice. She didn't consider herself the breathy sort.

"Have we been introduced?" he asked with a frown. "I ought to be much more conversant about these things since I've shown up to the launches of two of my sisters, but none of the rules want to stick in my head."

Connie bit the inside of her cheek to prevent her amusement from spreading across her face.

"I think we were actually introduced very briefly when I made my debut at the same time as one of your sisters. Since this is a house party, I suppose the rules aren't nearly as stringent as in Town." She held out her hand to introduce herself. "It might be unusual, but I might as well remind you who I am." She almost stumbled over her words as his large, warm hand engulfed hers. From his attire he seemed to be a wellborn gentleman, but the calluses evident on his fingers and palm indicated he worked as a labourer. "I am Lady Constance Moreland."

The gentleman bowed over her hand, even placing a kiss on her wrist. A thrill shook through Constance's insides. Without gloves as she was that morning, it was a far different sensation than she was used to.

"It's a pleasure to remake your acquaintance Lady Constance Moreland. I am Florent, the Honorable Mr. Alcott, if we're being formal."

Connie blinked. This man was a conundrum. Dressed elegantly, but clearly a worker, he was the heir to the viscountcy next door. And Miss Alcott's oldest brother. The other late arriving guest because he couldn't be torn away from his estate. He was her exact opposite from what she had gleaned from people's chatter. So why was she so instinctively drawn to him?

He was a handsome man, of course, but she had met dozens of handsome men in the course of her life. None had ever made her wish to linger in their presence. It was a large part of why she had taken herself off to travel the world when Grandmother Asquith had left Constance her fortune. No, this was just an aberration of the air here at Everleigh, Connie assured herself as she finally pulled her hand out of the man's clasp and took another step back, using the excuse of executing a curtsy to put a little more distance between them.

"I hadn't heard that you had arrived, Mr. Alcott," Constance finally blurted out and instantly coloured. She never blurted. It was the most absurd reaction. She tried to make a recovery. "How are things at Alcott?"

"Well, thank you. We are having a quiet moment, so I listened to my mother's urgings to get out of the house, even if it was only to next door." He grinned. "Does it not seem a trifle strange to be packing and attending a house party a mere twenty-minute ride away?" He asked the question while shaking his head. "But my mother and Lady Adelaide both insisted that I needed to stay over if I was to attend at all. And I suppose, it would be tiresome to be riding back and forth, especially in the dark or if it were to rain."

"And you would, no doubt, miss out on some of the experience of it all," Constance added with a gentle smile.

"Are you having an experience, my lady?" Florent asked with a chuckle that sent another thrill through her.

"Everything is an experience, my lord," she countered, lifting her chin lest he start thinking anything questionable about her.

"I suppose that is true," he replied, a slight frown crinkled his forehead as he watched her attentively. "Ought I not to have asked? I meant it to be a jest, but it seems to have offended you."

Constance blinked and heat filled her chest and face. He had obviously not been intending any sort of implication. He probably didn't even know anything about her if he didn't go about much in Society. She shouldn't have been so quick to take offense. She owed him an apology, but she didn't know how to do it without telling him why she had been so touchy.

"No apologies needed, my lord. Or rather, it is on my side to do so. I think I must have slept fitfully and didn't awaken fit for company it would seem."

"Not at all," he murmured, bowing to her slightly once more. "I say, have you seen either my mother or my sister? That's Lady Alcott and Miss Alcott if you don't know who I'm connected to."

Constance was instantly charmed. While, as a nobleman, he ought to be better informed about who everyone was, he didn't expect everyone to know who he was either. Somehow, she appreciated that quality since even on the continent who was who was a very important topic.

But Connie had just been wondering about Daisy and was already worrying the girl was getting up to shenanigans. It was a common occurrence at some house parties. Constance doubted Lady Adelaide would appreciate her guests loosening themselves to that extent, but Connie didn't want to stir up any trouble for the young woman.

"I've just left the salon and didn't see either of your family members there. But it is a very large house so I cannot be certain where anyone is. I'm, in fact, looking for my companion as well."

"Did I hear tell that Miss Smith is your companion? I believe I might have seen her in my wanderings."

Connie tried not to stare but how did the man know her companion and yet it had been necessary for him to be introduced to her? A frown started to crease her forehead but Constance exerted a concerted effort at stopping its formation.

She had been uncomfortable with the other guests and was dreading the next rumoured arrival. Mr. Alcott was causing her strange impulses. It was all rather absurd. She needed to find Peggy in order to prevent herself from stepping into trouble. It was strange that both Miss Alcott and Miss Smith were missing. She only hoped trouble hadn't found them while searching for her.

"How helpful," she murmured. "Or rather, it would be helpful if you could recall where it was that you encountered her."

Florent grinned. "She was with Lady Adelaide in the foyer when I arrived."

"Oh, are you that literally just arrived?"

"That literally," he agreed with a nod. "I was busy throughout the entire day yesterday, so it was well into the evening when I finally could have come over. I decided one more night of sleep in my own bed would be preferable, besides the fact that it might be slightly less rude to arrive in the morning rather than the late evening when I was already late anyway."

Constance grinned. "And since the travel was so extensive, it must have been a trial," she added with a teasing grin. To her delight, Florent did not appear to take the least offence. He returned her grin.

"Isn't that always the way? I suppose since you had the furthest to come, you were probably the first one here."

"Actually, I believe that honour goes to your mother and sister. I was actually another late arrival, only having arrived here yesterday."

"Oh, well, then the viscountess shan't mind me overly, in that case. I haven't thrown out her numbers for days on end as my mother would like me to think."

Connie smiled anew. "Just last night, but it didn't seem to bother Lady Adelaide overmuch."

"I appreciate your saying so. I will use you as a witness if I must."

"I don't think so, I'm afraid, my lord. I shouldn't like to get between a man and his mother."

Florent's eyebrow rose as he regarded her with interest. "I beg your pardon, my lady."

Heat flooded Constance from the top of her head to at least the pit of her belly and she knew no amount of effort would be able to keep the red from filling her face. She hadn't meant to imply anything other than not wishing to become entangled in a family dispute, but she could see how her words could have been taken to mean something far more complicated and not at all what she had intended.

"Thank you for the information about Miss Smith. I will see you later." With those abrupt words, Constance turned on her heel and fled. It was fleeing in her mind even if it was at a gentle, sedate pace that would appear to be unexceptional to any observer, even the confounding man who seemed to be staring holes into her back as she walked away from him.

But Constance hadn't been able to deal with the expression on his face. It had been the strangest combination of interest, fascination, flirtation, and appreciation. All varying degrees of expressions she had witnessed on the faces of other gentlemen many times before. But she had never been affected in the same way before. She had never been inclined to linger and bask in the attention. And yet she had done so many times. Constance Moreland was not a fleer. It was the exact opposite of her personality. Except for that one time when they had been informed that a battle was about to break out near them, then one could consider that she had fled. But normally Constance was the type to take a firm stand, not run away from uncomfortable situations.

When one considered it, her entire life was an uncomfortable situation. She was young, unwed, reasonably attractive, and sufficiently well off to be considered independently wealthy. And she chose to travel the world with a companion in tow. And yet she had managed to never court a single scandal aside from her very own existence. Her companion's reputation for being a stickler for propriety was one reason no hint of scandal had ever settled upon her, which was probably partially why she was so unsettled by her companion's absence.

The other reason was that she had never before been tempted to linger in a gentleman's company. *Why now? Why this gentleman?*

She had meant to try to keep Mr. Alcott occupied in order to prevent him from looking for his sister, Connie remembered too late. The urge to turn back was ignored. Miss Alcott would have to fend for herself for now. Lady

Constance needed to recover from her first encounter with the Honorable Mr. Alcott.

Chapter Two

W*hat an interesting woman.* The thought entered and exited Florent's mind as he watched her scurry away. From what he had heard of her, he never would have expected to witness such an event. He didn't think Lady Constance Moreland, world travelling debutante, would do anything that even somewhat resembled running away.

But it had definitely looked to Florent as though she were in a great hurry to get away from him. He probably should feel insulted. But instead, he was amused. As the oldest of six children and the brother to three sisters, he was well aware of the vagaries of humans, especially the females of the species.

That thought made him roll his eyes and shake his head. His mother used language like that. Lady Alcott thought of herself as an amateur botanist. She was forever talking about characteristics and species. It was also how he and all his siblings ended up with strange flower-related names.

Speaking of his mother, he really ought to find her so he could present himself as the obedient son she wanted to think him, despite the fact that he was advancing in years considerably past the schoolroom age of needing to obey his mother. In fact, if not for his being the heir, he would have moved out of his family's home years ago. He envied Lady Constance her life of leisurely travel. He couldn't relate to it in the least, but he fought a sense of jealousy that she had such a luxury.

Of course, she might not see it that way. Well, obviously, unless she was the verist dolt, she would recognize that she had been afforded a luxury and a privilege that few could enjoy, especially not young ladies. It was quite commonplace for young gentlemen to do the Grand Tour. And he would have done so as well even as the heir, except that the estate had gone into decline right around the time that he ought to have been planning his Tour. He had chosen to forego his trip in order to remain and help his father right the path the estate was on. And then he had never been able to get away after that. The estate needed him. Or maybe that's just what he told himself as the dream of travelling slipped further and further from his grasp.

Now he was a grown man who probably ought to start considering starting his own family, and he had barely even left the county he had been born in, let alone having even left the country. It was a lowering sensation. And one he was not going to dwell upon that day. His mother would never forgive him. He had finally arrived, late, but present. He couldn't compound his dastardly behavior of being tardy by also woolgathering about opportunities he had missed.

But perhaps Lady Constance would be willing to tell him a little bit about her experiences. If she were a good enough storyteller, it might just feel like he had been there himself.

Florent nearly snorted. No one was that good a storyteller. But it would have to do. And he had to stop thinking about it for now as he sought out his family members.

He remembered well the layout of Everleigh, but Florent suspected the houseguests would be using the house in a much different way than he and his brothers had done as boys playing with the Earl of Everleigh's sons. As youngsters, they had stayed far from the fashionable areas of the house out of fear of breaking something during their roughhousing. Of course, he had seen every room in the exceedingly large house, but he was still a trifle concerned about getting lost in the proper section of the large building. And no self-respecting nobleman wanted to ask the footmen for directions. But the servants were sure to know where his mother and sister were. And he couldn't exactly start searching the entire house.

"I say, could you please tell me where I might find Lady Alcott? Or Miss Alcott?"

The footman appeared dismayed by the question, which brought a frown to Florent's face. It shouldn't have been a difficult question.

"Alcott?"

The voice came from behind him, not from the footman, who still hadn't answered his question. Florent turned toward the one who'd called him.

"My lord," he exclaimed in greeting, bowing to the owner of this grand edifice. "I haven't seen you in a dog's age.

The old earl chuckled over Florent's exclamation, as had been Florent's intention. It had been one of the earl's favorite expressions when the brothers had all been boys.

"I didn't think you were going to attend." The earl had always had a way of making him feel like a recalcitrant school boy even as he had grown into manhood. This was one of those times.

"I couldn't get away until now," he tried to excuse but the earl only made a slightly disapproving humming noise as though he didn't want to outright disagree with a guest. Which was actually very restrained of the old codger, and Florent appreciated it.

"Well, you're here now so you might as well come and join the rest of Amelia's guests. I don't know what I was thinking to let that girl fill the place up with visitors. But she seems to be having a good time, so I suppose that's why."

Florent blinked over the older man's convoluted rambling but nodded anyway and fell into step with his noble neighbour.

"So what was such a riveting situation that you couldn't leave it with the servants?" Everleigh asked with a grumble in his tone.

"Foaling," Florent answered briefly, bringing the earl's scold to a sudden conclusion.

"Ah, I see," Everleigh replied, seemingly in agreement that this was an acceptable excuse. "Did it end well?"

"Yes, mothers and babies are all well, thank you, my lord." Florent paused, deciding not to start raving about the beautiful animals as would be his first inclination. "And how are you managing here with your guests?"

"Amelia is keeping everyone in line at least, so they aren't interfering too much with the running of the estate. Of course, she has taken to running the estate, so I'm not sure how she is managing both, but the house hasn't fallen down in the last few days, so I suppose she must be doing it right."

Florent snickered. He couldn't help himself. He wasn't sure if the earl had meant to be amusing but Florent hadn't been able to keep his amusement completely contained. Fortunately, when the earl glanced at him, despite the frown wrinkling his brow,

Florent could see the old man's eyes were twinkling with his own amusement.

"And surely Everleigh shan't fall apart in a fortnight anyhow," Florent added after he was able to stem his amusement.

"If Adelaide did one thing right in his life, it was finding that girl and getting her to agree to marry him."

Florent snorted again. He rather suspected Amelia might have done the finding, but he wasn't going to argue with the earl. He was happy for his friend. And if truth be told, even a little envious. Florent wasn't sure how he was supposed to find a wife of his own since he had taken over the running of the estate several years ago and was still working to pull it out of the downward spiral his father and grandfather had allowed it to get into. He was almost there, but it had taken his full concentration for nearly a decade since he had finished school. While his friends had all been kicking up a lark in Town or on their Tour, he had been at Alcott learning animal husbandry and crop management. The earl had actually helped him considerably. He owed his sister's generous dowry to the Earl of Everleigh's excellent advice because Lord Alcott, Florent's own father, had depleted every account in an effort to hide the truth of the family's situation.

Now there was nothing to hide. Alcott was thriving. But Florent felt as though he had been turned into a steward and left behind. He had barely even been to Town but for very brief visits during his first two sisters' Seasons, let alone travelling anywhere else, unlike Lady Constance. He hadn't even gone up for any of his youngest sister, Daisy's, Season. So now that he finally felt in the clear, he wanted to make it up to the girl. She was such a great sport most of the time. She'd never complained about his outward lack of interest in her. Florent was afraid that might be because she was so used to it, but he ignored that possibility. She was more than a decade younger than he and probably didn't remember when he was young and entertaining. That would have to change too, he supposed.

"I say, my lord, have you seen my sister? I've just arrived and I was hoping to spend some time with her."

Everleigh frowned at the question. "Why would you want to spend time with your sister? Most men run the other way, from my observations."

Florent smiled. "I've done that far too much of late," he said. "It's time for a different tack."

Everleigh harumphed. "Come along, the girl ought to be with everyone else right now, which is where we were heading anyway."

"Have you been able to spend any time with the girl? Does she seem to be having a good time?"

Everleigh turned a fierce look upon him from under his scruffy eyebrows. Florent had to stifle the grin that wanted to spread across his face. He was certain that look would have terrified him as a boy, which was probably its intent.

"Do you really expect me to have any insights into a young woman's thoughts, boy? We've known each other since you were a scrubby child. Surely you ought to know better than that."

Florent finally did allow the grin to spread, but he also nodded at the earl's words. "You are right, it was a foolish question. I'll just ask her myself when we find her."

"You do that," Everleigh growled, but Florent suspected there was good humour behind the bristle. "And you're probably right to keep an eye on her. Amelia seems to have turned her attention to match making but wasn't as cautious as I'd like in her guest list."

Florent frowned over the earl's final statement. How odd. He would have expected Amelia to be very careful in her choosing. He was under the impression she was trying to find his sister a match, since his mother had failed to do so. He almost quickened his pace but checked himself with the earl at his side. He couldn't very well drag the older gentleman along behind him.

They finally arrived at a large receiving room that at first glance appeared to be overflowing with well-dressed people. For a brief moment Florent actually checked at the door, wondering if he were sufficiently attired. Along with not having gone to Town in an age came not having kept up with fashion in the least. But Florent was certain his valet had done sufficiently so that he wouldn't bring shame upon himself or his hosts. It was unlike him to suffer any qualms of insecurity like this. If he ever felt inadequate at Alcott, he ignored the sensation as it was unlikely to help him reach his goals for the place. This was probably no different.

Not that he really had any goals for this visit. To his mind, he was just being neighbourly. When one's biggest neighbour invited you to their party, you really ought to accept. And when said party was the first one that was being thrown there in twenty years, you'd best believe you had to be there all the more so. Florent knew he'd be getting an earful from his mother about arriving late as it was. But what was he supposed to do about the horses?

"You leave it to the servants, you gudgeon," his found mama insisted when he finally found her. "I'm embarrassed that you've only just strolled in at this late date."

"Don't be, Mother. I'm a grown man. My actions no longer reflect upon you. Besides, I wrote to Lady Adelaide keeping her updated on my situation."

"Your actions will never cease to reflect upon me," Lady Alcott insisted. "And you ought to have apprised me as well as our hostess. I'm your mother."

Florent again found himself suppressing laughter. It was the most cheerful he had felt in probably years. It made him feel light and young. Was this what debutantes felt like? *Probably not.* He shook his head at the silly thought.

"What have you been spending your time with while you've been here thus far, Mother?"

"Worrying about you, for one thing." If you wanted to complain about Lady Alcott, one of the things you could mention was that she didn't easily let a matter drop, that was for certain, Florent thought as he tried very hard not to roll his eyes at her latest comment.

"And besides that?" he prompted when she didn't continue.

"Renewing old friendships," she finally said, relenting in her disapproving attitude. "Lord and Lady Bathurst are here with their sweet young daughter." She paused and turned a speculative expression upon her son. "I say, now that you're here, you should think about Lady Isabelle. She would make a fine wife for you."

"I am here to relax, Mother, not get matchmade."

"You could do both," she insisted with a bit of a harumph which made Florent actually guffaw.

"I think they might be mutually exclusive for a gentleman, my lady, I'm sorry to say."

His mother grumbled under her breath once more but didn't bother to argue the matter further. She merely tucked her arm more firmly into his elbow and continued to stroll at his side.

"You mustn't be cross with me, my dear son, but I haven't been keeping a very close eye upon your sister this week. I couldn't even begin to tell you what she has been up to except that I have seen her dancing in the evening and of course, at most meals."

"Have you lost your mind?" Florent asked, his tone good-natured despite the tenor of his question. His mother laughed as was his intention.

"It would seem so, wouldn't it? But I don't think I have. I'm just tired of chaperoning, to be honest. And with her friends here, I figured she didn't really need me to watch over her so closely as she would in Town. Since you've taken over everything else at Alcott, perhaps you ought to take over seeing after Daisy. She wears me out. And I've been having far too much amusement while catching up with Lady Bathurst."

"Who is Lady Bathurst to you? Why would you be so in her pocket that you weren't watching over Daisy?"

"Don't scold me, Florent. You know how Daisy has become. Half the time she wants to be off exploring, the other half she acts as though she is already a matron. I've tried to tell her she needed to be a trifle less serious about it all, and she sent me away with a flea in my ear."

Florent grinned over her use of the cant expression but he didn't interject, hoping she would elaborate a bit more. His patience was rewarded.

"Would you believe, that wild Northcott son, the one who has been traipsing all over the colonies, he had a talk with her about how she was carrying on, and it seemed to affect her more than anything I've been saying."

"Really?" Florent asked. "I thought she hated Foster ever since she was twelve or thirteen."

Lady Alcott made a non-committal expression. "I thought so, too, but perhaps she got over it."

Florent frowned. He didn't really see his sister as the sort who got over that degree of emotions, but who was he to argue the subject?

"Have you made any other new friendships while you've been here? You didn't actually tell me anything about Lady Bathurst, either."

His mother giggled. He had never heard her make such a sound before. Florent wasn't sure what to make of the strange occurrence. It would seem the older woman was ready to reclaim her youth now that her youngest daughter was nearly launched.

"She was my best friend when I went to school briefly before I made my debut. And we debuted together. But then Bathurst is far away and there's only so much that can be said in a letter and when your house is filling with children, you'd rather spend time with them than sitting down to write endless letters, so our friendship waned over time. Now she's in Town with her youngest as am I, and we've renewed the acquaintance."

"Has Daisy become friends with their daughter?" Florent wondered how his sister was feeling about their mother's new distraction. He didn't have to wait long to learn some of it. His mother sighed.

"Daisy has not done well, I'm afraid to say. I think we shouldn't have bothered with a Season for her this year. It is the strangest thing, Flor. As I said, you should try talking to her."

"I?" Florent repeated with surprise. "She isn't likely to listen to me in matters of Society. I have woefully neglected her since she made her debut. And as you know I have barely set foot in Town. Surely I have no experience to share with her on this matter."

"Sure you do," his fond mother insisted. "You have always watched out for her. There were many occasions I could note. This is not much different."

Florent's eyebrows felt like they were receding into his hairline. "What would you have me talk to her about?" He did quite love his sister even if he couldn't imagine trying to direct her in this regard. In any regard, really. Their Daisy had a mind of her own.

"She seems to be trying too hard. The poor dear is determined to wed, but there haven't yet been any offers this year. I'm worried what will happen to her if she doesn't receive an offer." She paused for a moment before adding, "Actually, that was in Town. Here, she keeps absenting herself. I am not sure what she's up to, and I have been too preoccupied to pursue the topic. I also have no desire for unpleasantness. You know how she can be. You should do it."

Florent laughed. He loved his mother dearly, but he knew she was ready to retire from the position of chaperone. He had no idea how he was to talk to his sister on this topic, but he needed to find her first.

"I am not confident of my success in dealing with Daisy, but I will try to speak with her. When was the last time you saw her?"

"This morning," his mother replied promptly but too vaguely for Florent's comfort. "You are a dear, thank you, my boy."

Flor grinned again. He didn't feel like a boy. He hadn't done so since he'd finished school and started trying to turn his family's fortunes around. It had been more than a decade, but he was finally quietly confident that he had succeeded. He also felt old from the experience. He had hidden it from all his younger siblings. They thought he was an odd stick. He envied them their carefree youth. He hadn't had that experience but was glad he had been able to provide it for them, whether they acknowledged the fact or not.

After bowing over his mother's hand, Florent turned on his heel, ready to resume his responsibilities.

Chapter Three

"Have you found your family?" Constance called cheerfully, determined to ignore the strange sensations this man caused her and protect his sister from his attention. She knew full well he hadn't seen his sister, as she had been shamelessly eavesdropping. It was one of her favorite pastimes, one she viewed as completely harmless as she never misused the information she invariably discovered. But she did love to see people's reactions when she had more information than they expected of her.

"My mother seems to be quite enjoying herself," he commented in lieu of a proper response. Constance found she respected his answer.

"I am still in search of my companion. Shall we stroll together?"

It was an uncharacteristically bold invitation, but Constance kept her expression as innocent as she could manage, fighting a blush. She didn't want the handsome gentleman to think she was offering anything less savoury than a stroll in search of their quarries. While she intended to prevent him from searching for his sister it wasn't for any morally ambiguous reasons.

Well, she hesitated even in her own thoughts, it actually was, but not for her own pursuits, she excused. Constance had become a keen observer in her years of pursuing spinsterhood. It had served her well and never failed to keep her entertained. Except this time, she was reasonably sure she might be about to aid in the ruination of a gently bred young woman. But she was tired of her own current situation, she certainly didn't want to help another woman join her eccentric spinster status.

"Tell me about Alcott," she urged the gentleman, taking his elbow with a smile as Mr. Alcott appeared to be struggling to keep the frown from his face. He likely thought her an imbecile.

"What would you like to know?" Now Constance could hear amusement in his voice even though she was no longer looking at him. She found she couldn't meet his eyes and attempt to deceive him, so she ensured her gaze was kept firmly elsewhere.

"Everything," she declared rather dramatically and just managed not to roll her eyes.

Constance was being ridiculous and couldn't seem to stop herself. She had witnessed debutantes being equally dramatic but had never thought she had it in her to be so. At the advanced age of nearly twenty-five, she had seen far too much of the world and the people who inhabited it to feel excitable about any of it.

She had begun to long for a small cottage by the sea, perhaps in Brighton, although she had heard that was starting to become fashionable since the Prince had decided to start building a place there for himself and his friends. She brought her attention back to the matter at hand. "Actually, do you know if there are any villages around here that would be safe enough for a spinster to take up residence?"

"Oh, I would imagine all of them would be," Mr. Alcott replied immediately. "Have you an aunt or some sort of connection who is looking to relocate?"

Constance laughed. "I was thinking of myself."

She could feel his stare. "You speak of yourself as a spinster?" He was so surprised he sounded almost incredulous. "You can't be that much older than my sister. Please don't let her hear you speaking like that."

"Oh, I'm sorry, but she already has. We had quite the conversation on the topic, to be truthful. She didn't seem overly enamoured with the idea, so I don't think you need to worry overmuch."

Connie got lost in thought for a moment remembering their conversation on the topic.

"I am so envious of you, my lady," the younger woman had nearly gushed when they were seated together on a settee after supper the night before.

"You are? That is not the usual response I gain from most wellborn ladies."

The girl had trilled a laugh. "That is most odd. I think most just don't want to admit they're jealous."

"So, you'd like to be a travelling spinster?"

"Oh no, not in the least," she'd answered promptly, adding in a slight shudder for effect. "I am determined that I shall wed soon. But I would also like to have adventures such as you are surely having."

Connie had been about to ask the other woman if that was why she had gone haring off by herself that afternoon, but they had been interrupted before she could do so. Besides the fact that she was unsure how to politely ask another woman if she was intentionally courting scandal.

Florent's words brought her back to the present.

"I'm not worried she will wish to follow your lead. I'm worried she will become even more determined to find her husband this Season. A determined Daisy can be rather reckless," he said with what appeared to be a shudder, making Constance have to bite the inside of her lip to keep herself from laughing. "There was this time when she was quite little that she found someone had thrown a bag of kittens into the lake on our property. She didn't know how to swim, but that didn't cross her mind when she leapt into the water to save the creatures. Of course, I had to jump in after her to save them all."

"That was brave of you," Constance cooed. She actually cooed. No human should coo, she reprimanded herself fiercely. That ought to be left for the pigeons and doves. She just barely managed not to roll her eyes again.

He didn't seem to notice her foolishness, though. Perhaps women cooed over him all the time. She wouldn't be surprised. He was handsome and eligible, being the heir to his father's viscountcy. It was unusual that the title and the family name were the same, but she quite liked it. It made them seem all the more like family. Unlike her. There was only her and one brother with her name since her sisters had wed and her older brother, their father's heir, had a courtesy title. It made her feel all the more isolated than she already was as a spinster travelling the world with her companion.

"Not really, anyone would have done it."

Constance blinked having lost the thread of the conversation when she had allowed her mind to drift. She had to think for a beat to remember what he was responding to. "Perhaps not anyone. The individual who had thrown the kittens in probably wouldn't have."

"If he valued his employment, he would have," Florent insisted. "But we never did find out who had been so cruel. And believe me, Daisy certainly tried."

Constance laughed and then nodded slightly. She had been debating with herself whether or not she ought to get involved, but this gentleman had just confirmed her impression of his sister. While Constance couldn't fully approve of clandestine meetings for young ladies, if Daisy wanted to pursue a dalliance or whatever had her traipsing about looking furtive, Constance wasn't going to stand in her way, nor was she going to assist Daisy's brother in interfering either.

It might be considered a little bold of her, but she continued at his side with her hand in Mr. Alcott's elbow. He hadn't really invited her presence, but she was going to give it to him anyway and hope he didn't notice that no one knew where Daisy might be.

"So, tell me about Alcott," she invited again.

"Surely you don't really want to hear about an old country estate after you've had the opportunity to see all there has been to see wherever you've been," Florent protested, accepting her arm with a smile and a pat and allowing her to steer them toward the front receiving room. "I ought to be prompting you to tell me all about your travels."

"Well, that might be far more boring, I'm afraid."

"Never say so. I've been fantasizing for years about travelling the world. Don't dash my imaginings with telling me you didn't enjoy them."

Constance smiled but lifted one of her shoulders with an awkward expression. "Fine then, I won't tell you," She added with a laugh, "No, I cannot honestly say it hasn't been lovely. I have found it wonderful to visit all the places we often only get a chance to read about. And many more I had never even heard of before. It would be disingenuous of me to claim otherwise. But I suppose one is always fascinated with what we don't know. I don't know what it's like to live on a country estate, especially not as a man who gets to run it. I think there would be a steadiness in that which I find sorely lacking in my travels."

Florent kept walking at a steady pace and continued to keep his left hand over hers where it rested in the crook of his elbow. Constance thought he had done it out of habit. Perhaps his mother or sisters walked with him like that. But she found a slight thrill from it anyway. It made her feel safe and cherished in a way she'd never felt before. And a little thrill shot through her that wasn't exactly comfort. She tried to ignore the sensations since it was most likely not real in the first place. She noticed he also had an expression of concentration on his face as though he were pondering what she had just said.

"I think you might have just settled upon what causes most people's restlessness. What others have is always better than what you have until you get it for yourself. I guess that is why one ought to cultivate contentment. Otherwise, you'll always be chasing after what you don't have."

Constance couldn't quite agree. "Or you need to realize quickly enough that what you thought you wanted isn't actually for you."

"But some things are rather too permanent for changing your mind, wouldn't you say?"

Constance tilted her head in question, and he continued.

"For example, if you had wed when you first made your debut rather than deciding to start travelling when you received your inheritance, wouldn't you have always wondered? If you were married and started having children, you wouldn't be able to traipse all about the continent."

"It's not so very difficult to travel, even with children, in my opinion," Constance protested.

"A gentleman with lands and crops and tenants might not feel the same way."

Constance wanted to stare at Mr. Alcott to try to read his feelings behind his statement. She heard so many conflicting emotions in his tone as he made that last statement. Did he regret his choices? Was he envious of hers? Or censorious? It was terribly hard to tell. She rather thought it was all those feelings rolled together. Poor man. But she could somewhat relate. She had extremely mixed feelings about her own life choices. She tried not to sigh. She couldn't seem to escape those unhelpful thoughts.

Perhaps she just needed to decide on somewhere even more adventurous to travel to rather than settling down in her longed for cottage. Travel on the continent was so common today, there was no longer anything eccentric about it. Perhaps she ought to travel in the other direction next time. The New World would be a better destination for her. She almost wrinkled her nose at the thought. America seemed rather too traitorous to her but from what she had heard of the Canadas, they were even further from civilized. And the travel to Botany Bay just might kill her. Months on a boat would be primitive and uncomfortable no matter how deep your pockets might be.

She needed to turn the topic and think of her own pursuits later.

"If you didn't have your lands and crops and such to be concerned about, where would you like to travel?"

She smiled as he tried to sputter that he hadn't meant himself in his comments, but Connie knew he didn't really mean it. Finally, he simmered down and thought the matter through.

"A part of me is captivated with the thought of any of the colonies. It must be fascinating to see people starting new lives completely from nothing. I've read tales of men buying a tract of land and needing to fell the trees necessary to build their houses, then clear the land for crops and animals. I cannot imagine the amount of work that would be required but the sense of accomplishment if one succeeded must make it all worthwhile."

Constance nodded. "I wonder how many actually succeed, though."

"What do you mean?"

"As you said, the amount of work seems unimaginable to me. What do they do for food in the interim? When they cannot plant anything to feed themselves or their animals. And how far from a merchant would you be if it is a completely and thoroughly undeveloped piece of land? It would be difficult to even purchase the food you might need. And where do you live while you're felling the trees?" Constance suppressed a shudder. While she needed to figure out what else to do with herself, she knew that wasn't going to be it.

To her surprise, though, Florent laughed. "I see your point and cannot disagree. But you might note I didn't say I actually wanted to do those things. I have no intention of throwing off my inheritance to run away to the colonies. But I would like to witness it, I think. To see what people have accomplished and how. Perhaps speak with them. That would be fascinating, wouldn't you think?"

"I do think it would be, yes. Perhaps I will head West instead of East on my next foray of travelling."

Florent's hand tightened slightly where it was still settled over hers in the crook of his arm. "Does your family not worry over you? I am surprised they allow you such free rein."

She was now certain she could hear censure in his tone. Constance almost pulled her hand out of his but it felt so lovely in his warm grasp she couldn't quite bring herself to do it. He must have sensed her disquiet, though as he patted her hand gently before settling once more. "I suppose I just insulted you, didn't I?" Florent asked with a low chuckle. "I do apologize, my lady. That was certainly not my intention. But thinking about my own sister, I don't suppose denying her would have any effect especially if she had the means to accomplish her aims as I've heard you do. But surely, they must worry immensely about you. All the more if you were to begin ocean travel."

"Yes, I imagine there must be a little more risk in ocean travel than what I have been doing, but I cannot say that my family troubles themselves terribly over me. It seemed to be a relief to them when I was no longer on their hands on a daily basis. Now they can comfortably shake their heads about my choices without needing to actually bestir themselves."

From the corner of her eye, Constance could see that Florent had started to frown. Her words were not sitting comfortably with him.

"That cannot possibly be true," Mr. Alcott said, shaking his head.

Constance laughed and squeezed his arm. She didn't wish to argue with him on the topic, but she was certain she was correct. "Never mind about that, now tell me, which of the colonies would you wish to see first if given the choice?"

To her relief, he seemed to accept her turn of the topic and she relaxed by his side as he pondered her question.

"I wonder if Bombay might be the most exotic choice as it is so very different from anywhere I'm familiar with. That might be the greatest adventure."

Constance nodded. “True, but the greatest adventure might also be the greatest challenge. For your first foray into adventure, it might be best not to have it be too grand.”

She felt, rather than saw, his shrug. “But this is mere fantasy anyway, so it needn’t matter how impractical I might be.”

Constance laughed again. “That is true. Very well, my lord, our imaginary entourage shall set off for Bombay. What do you expect we shall see?”

“Any manner of things that I cannot even begin to imagine, I suppose. Elephants, I would think, would be the first thing I’d hope to see.”

Constance wrinkled her nose. “Even if you can escape your animals at home, you still wish to see more. Do you suppose that’s a male trait?”

Florent laughed. “No doubt. So, if the creatures aren’t your interest, what do you hope to see?”

“The fabrics,” she answered immediately. “And the sunshine. I’ve discovered that light seems different in various places. It has quite fascinated me. I am not the most scientific person so I cannot tell you why it is the case. I’ve thought it might be the heat, but I’m not sure how that would corelate. But sunlight or the sky or what have you, looks different in each locale. I enjoy that quite immensely. So, it is what I most like to observe in each place I visit. And I would expect, being that far from the familiar, it might be the most different.”

“Now I am all the more determined that one day I will go somewhere.” Constance’s heart squeezed slightly at the sound of disappointment ringing in his voice. While she sometimes lamented her nomadic life, she could see that others might envy her for it. “Where have you seen the best light, my lady? Where would you recommend I start my adventuring?”

"Oh, what a lovely question. I will have to ponder a moment." She didn't really have to think about it. Constance would never forget the experience. But she didn't want to make him feel any more housebound than he already did. And she deeply appreciated the sense of gratitude this conversation was giving her for her own circumstances. Besides, the longer she kept him preoccupied, the more time Miss Alcott had to get herself out of any potential trouble. Constance so enjoyed being able to accomplish many things at once.

"I would say the best light I've enjoyed was on a mountain in Helvetia. It took a great deal of effort to get to the rustic accommodations we visited but it was worth every strain."

"Hmm," Florent responded. "Wasn't that a risk seeing as Napoleon has been showing such an interest in that region?"

Connie shrugged. "Maybe a little, but it was definitely worth it."

He didn't look convinced, but he nodded and said, "Thank you. I will read about it."

Constance laughed. "You've changed your mind already?" she accused questioningly. "You've just agreed that you needed some adventure."

Florent shook his head. "I want educated adventure, my dear lady. I cannot change in a twinkling from never having been anywhere to running off into the night. I will read about this Helvetia and research the best way to get there before I set out. I would imagine a mountaintop could get very cold. It wouldn't do for me to be traipsing about in the dead of winter, would it?"

Constance grinned. "I suppose not, but it would certainly be adventurous."

"And likely to put me off any future endeavours."

"That's true. You are wiser than me, Mr. Alcott." An errant thought had her wistfully thinking it would be nice to spend more time in this wise man's company, but she promptly chased the ridiculous thought away.

Chapter Four

"Have you ever been put off your travels by your experiences thus far?"

The way the lady laughed and shook her head and lifted one shoulder in half a shrug led Florent to believe she didn't really know the answer to his question. Or that the answer was complicated. He kept his hand over hers steady and held his tongue hoping she'd elaborate in words rather just in reactions. His patience would be rewarded eventually, he was sure.

For some reason, he was suspicious of her spending time by his side. She was a beautiful woman and far more interesting than any he had ever met, not just because she was considered an eccentric spinster despite not being much older than his sister. He rather thought she had probably been interesting long before that. They had been introduced the one time he had gone to Town for his first sister's debut. And he had definitely noticed her, even then although she would have probably been much like all the others making their curtsy to the queen that year. He had also never forgotten her despite how chaotic his life had been since.

Even out in the backwaters of Kent County they still got the gossip papers. Lady Alcott loved to stay abreast of the goings on in Town even if she didn't enjoy going for the Season unless it was necessary. She didn't want to feel behind when she did get there. So, she always knew the gossip. And she liked nothing more than to share it with her family as though she knew what she was talking about.

Lady Constance sighed. Florent had outwaited her, he was sure.

"Put off would be stating it much too strongly," she finally said with another tinkle of laughter that sounded like the chime of a bell. Florent liked it and hoped to hear it again even though he thought she might be uncomfortable. He kept a steady pace hoping she would elaborate. She sighed again, lightly.

"I don't find I like feeling unsettled." She said it as though she were uttering a deep, dark secret. Florent wanted to laugh but he knew that would end any further confidences.

"I can imagine that can't be pleasant," Florent replied mildly, hoping she would go into further detail.

It did prompt another tinkle of laughter from her. "No, not pleasant, you're right. I don't suppose you can relate, though, can you?"

Florent finally looked her in the face and offered her a mild smile. "There is very little about my life that isn't settled," he agreed with her, although he wasn't being perfectly truthful. It was almost there but things had been decidedly unsettled for years. He was only now finally seeing the success of his efforts after more time than he had ever expected. He didn't like feeling unsettled either. He was certain they weren't speaking about the same type of experience, though, so he didn't bother to tell her about it. Not that she had asked.

"Does your life feel unsettled because you travel from place to place? Or because you don't know where you will go next?"

"It's just so very rootless," she exclaimed, again as though it were a secret that had been pulled out of her. "And everyone thinks it's marvelous or scandalous or some other superlative that isn't really true. I've done nothing scandalous except be different from others." She grew silent at his side for a moment before adding, "It's not as though I want to be like everyone else. I certainly don't. But I also don't wish to feel like a spectacle, either. Like everyone is watching me and analyzing my actions in order to judge them."

"No, that sounds perfectly dreadful."

She smiled in appreciation and for a moment Florent's chest swelled as though he had performed some great feat. It was ridiculous but true. He wished to continue to experience the sensation.

"Tell me about Alcott," she invited once more, in a softer tone, as though she sincerely wished to know. Again, Florent had the strangest sensation.

"We are trying our hand at cotton for the first time this year."

"Cotton? I'm clearly not an experienced grower of plants, but won't that be difficult in this climate?"

Florent grinned over the question. No woman fancied herself a botanist like his mother, thus his and his siblings' odd names, but he liked that Lady Constance was very frank about her own knowledge or lack thereof. But she was actually well informed. Not that he had discussed the matter with many, but whenever he had ever mentioned his crops to anyone they had invariably smiled and nodded in polite disinterest and carried on to discuss something else. He appreciated that this woman at least had an intelligent question to ask.

"That's a good question, my lady. We shall soon see. Some have been working to develop hardier seeds so that our wet weather won't be a problem, but really only trying it will prove the matter one way or the other."

She frowned slightly. "How risky is it for you?"

Again, Florent was impressed with her sensible question although it was verging on the over personal. He wasn't sure he wanted to confide in anyone on the subject, let alone a young lady he was barely acquainted with.

He lifted one shoulder and hoped his smile was slightly mysterious. He might have done what he'd intended, but it did not have the affect he'd hoped for. Constance's frown deepened despite the light laugh she uttered.

"You either don't quite know or you don't want to tell me." She smiled, revealing she wasn't in the least offended. "I cannot blame you. It was almost unforgivably rude to ask, wasn't it? I do apologize. Sometimes I forget that my quest for knowledge isn't normal."

Florent laughed with her. "Let's just say it's not usual, rather than it's abnormal. Most wouldn't even think to ask questions."

Her frown creased her forehead once more. "That's just because everyone is so terribly self centered," she said sadly, making Florent wonder what she had experienced to give her that knowledge. He supposed it might be that no one really cared all that much about her travels.

"Have you met my sister? She likes to ask questions." Of course, she had, he reminded himself, feeling a little silly. She was too beautiful for him to converse with comfortably. And she was just different enough that he rather hoped Daisy didn't become attached to her. He couldn't help thinking Lady Constance wouldn't be the best influence upon his youngest sister.

"I've met a couple of your sisters, as a matter of fact. You do realize one of them is here at the party, don't you?" She laughed again, the tinkle of bells that sounded so joyful and Florent once more hoped to prolong the moment no matter how unwise it might be to spend too much time with the exotic creature. "But of course, you do, you have already asked if I've seen her. Do forgive me, Mr. Alcott. My brain got stuck on our previous topic."

Florent smiled. She truly was a different sort.

"Ah, there she is now," Lady Constance surprised him by pointing over her shoulder. Florent quickly turned, losing the grasp he'd had on her hand as she slipped it from the crook of his elbow. How had she known who was coming behind them? Constance Moreland was a fascinating woman.

Florent got caught up in the flurry of activity that surrounded his energetic sister who exclaimed over his presence.

"I didn't think we'd ever see you here, Flor. It's good to see you. How is Father? And Alcott? Mama said something about lambs or foals or something?"

Even as he listened to Daisy, Florent heard the tinkle of Constance's laughter as she drifted away from them. He wondered if she was amused that Daisy hadn't even bothered to note which problem had kept him away. Florent shrugged internally. It was much the same as Lady Constance had remarked upon about other people's lack of attention. No one ever cared which problems he took care of as long as he did so without disturbing their peace. Even his father, the present Viscount Alcott, didn't much care what Florent did on the estate, merely appreciating that his heir managed to keep the family coffers full enough that he no longer had to concern himself with his own spend-thrift ways.

It was the way of things and Florent had stopped letting it bother him nearly a decade ago when he had first started taking over things, little by little. Now, in all but name, he was Viscount Alcott, and everyone in the county respected him as such. If he were to go anywhere else, he would be nothing but the Honorable Mr. Alcott. Not that there was anything wrong with that. He rather liked being called honorable. There was a certain ring to it. But there were times when he longed for the full authority the title would give him. If only it didn't require his father's death to achieve that position.

He tried not to sigh as he listened to his sister. Florent made an effort to focus on what she was telling him. It was unlike his baby sister to babble, but that was what was happening. If only their mother wasn't so caught up on her own pursuits. She ought to be more attentive to her youngest daughter or Daisy would end up an eccentric spinster like Lady Constance.

Not to say there was anything bad about Lady Constance. Florent quite liked what little he knew of her. But this was not the life he wanted for his sister. And he knew it wasn't the life Daisy wanted for herself. She struck him as an odd combination of independence and traditionalist. Unlike their other sisters, Daisy didn't even want a love match. But she definitely wanted a match. He needed to keep an eye on her so she didn't settle for just anyone. Even if she wasn't terribly concerned about loving the gentleman, there were certain criteria which would make him acceptable or not.

He pulled his circling thoughts back and tried to pay attention to his sister while also staring around the wide hallway at Everleigh. He needed to quickly ascertain who might be present and whether or not they were possibly good candidates for his sister's hand. He doubted her friends would have invited anyone unacceptable, but Florent didn't trust others to do the jobs he needed to see done himself.

He had told his mother he was at the house party to relax, but he could already see that was unlikely to happen. Between feeling strangely fascinated with Lady Constance and not wishing his sister to be equally intrigued while also hoping to keep his sister from any rash decisions, it wasn't probable to be restful.

But it would be interesting, he couldn't deny that.

Chapter Five

Constance found herself wanting to hover in the Alcotts' presence. It was terribly unlike her. Perhaps the time spent on the boat returning to England had addled her mind. Everything about her reactions these past couple of days had been unlike her. She didn't hate them; she just wasn't perfectly comfortable with them.

A farming, land-owning gentleman? When had she ever found one of those attractive? Especially one who had never left his own village? That was nearly anathema to her. He didn't even have a title at present. And yet walking with her hand in his elbow, while the most chaste of activities, had filled her belly with thrills she hadn't experienced in an age.

Perhaps she had eaten something off at lunch. She tried to console herself or convince herself, Constance wasn't sure which, but she knew, deep in her heart, that it was the steadiness of the gentleman that had somehow drawn her after the flightiness of the last couple of years. Perhaps it was true, you were always drawn back to your roots.

She had read somewhere that women were always drawn to men just like their fathers. Constance didn't think Mr. Alcott was anything like Lord Moore. But their circumstances struck her as similar.

Giving her head a slight shake that set her dark curls to dancing, Connie tried to put thoughts of gentlemen far from her mind. Reminding herself that she had only chatted with Mr. Alcott for so long because she had been endeavouring to keep him distracted so he wouldn't notice his sister's absence, but even she wasn't convinced that had remained true. It had been the allure of his steadiness. She could admit it to herself in the silence of her thoughts. But that was as far as it was going to go. She wasn't about to change her course at this late date. She quite liked being an eccentric nomad, she insisted even to herself.

Now it was time to find her straying companion and get on with being entertained.

When Constance finally found Miss Smith, she appeared to be deep in conversation with Lord Merton, one of their fellow guests. Connie lifted an eyebrow as Peggy's eyes rounded when they caught sight of her, as though she had been caught out doing something scandalous. Connie supposed, in a certain way, she was. Peggy ought to be keeping Connie company, not the viscount from the Bath region.

But Constance had known coming here was a risk. Peggy was tired of accompanying her around the continent. Her impoverished circumstances had made it necessary for her to accept the charitable position, but if she could snag a wealthy gentleman, she could settle down and have the life she'd always wanted.

The sinking in her stomach was to be ignored, Constance admonished herself. There were other impoverished cousins to embroil in her ventures. She had no intention of forcing anyone into her company. And really, her family ought to have ensured Peggy was provided for long before now. Or Connie should have seen to it herself.

And so it was that she did not march over to the duo and insist upon being included in their conversation. She also tried very hard not to stare and speculate. With that in mind, she approached the ladies gathered at the other end of the room. They appeared to be doing needlework, Constance realized too late. She despised the activity and had none of her own to contribute to the industriousness she observed.

"Do sit down, Lady Constance, and join us. We can send your girl or a footman to fetch your own projects, if you'd like."

Constance wasn't certain who the woman was referring to as her girl. If it was Peggy, Connie was all the more determined to allow her to marry out of her service to Constance. But if the woman meant her maid, it would beyond silly to call her down only to send her back up. Not that there was any needlework to be found in her rooms. Any repairs to her garments were performed by her maid. And since she had left home, she had never again picked up stitching of any sort. But she needn't admit to these harpies how she felt about the activity.

"Oh no, we needn't disturb anyone on my behalf. Perhaps one of you needs help sorting your threads or straightening your strings?" Connie hoped her smile wasn't too toothy or crooked or in any other way displaying the total lack of sincerity in her offer. Not that she wasn't sincere in her offer, it was just that she was instantly not enamoured with the ladies who seemed so determined to bend her to their form.

She quickly called herself to task within the confines of her own mind. She shouldn't paint them with the same brush as most she'd met. Constance prided herself as viewing people as individuals, just as she hoped people would view her. Perhaps the offer of fetching non-existent needlework from her room was a genuine lack of realization that there could be a lady who didn't have a stitching project on the go rather than an attempt at shaming her for not doing so.

"You could help me, if you have a mind to," her hostess, Lady Adelaide, called to her. "I am uncertain quite how I managed it, but my basket is nothing but a bundle of knots. If you have any skill at helping me detangle it, I would be so very grateful."

A grin struggled to stretch her face too wide for convention but Constance fought it as the women shuffled around so she could be seated next to their hostess' sister-in-law. "I'd be happy to help," Connie managed to say with a straight face. And it wasn't even a lie. She did love to help and she actually had quite a skill at detangling. It was just the seriousness of the assembled ladies that struck Connie's sense of absurd quite firmly. But she ignored the urge to giggle. It would get her ostracized instantly.

"So, as I was saying, my oldest daughter has finally presented her husband with his heir. After three daughters she was beginning to despair. A fine, healthy boy who is already wrapping his three sisters around his tiny little fingers, of course." Constance turned to watch Lady Alcott preen under the congratulations from the gathered women and had to fight her inappropriate amusement once more. Connie wondered how the woman thought this was any sort of accomplishment on her part. Although, she realized, that was particularly uncharitable of her in this instance. As her direct descendent, one could actually consider the child an extension of its grandmother so Connie accepted it was possible to consider congratulations in order.

"What have they named the boy?" she asked when it was her turn to say something. She thought it a reasonable question. She didn't know overmuch about babies but his size, weight, and health had already been discussed at length.

But the other ladies looked at her as though she were a simpleton.

"His name is a foregone conclusion, my dear," Lady Alcott finally responded. "Since he is the heir, of course."

Constance tried to keep her face as smooth as possible, but she was puzzled over the other woman's words. While Connie could accept that there would be titles the child would be saddled with at birth, did his given name need to be inherited as well? She supposed it didn't really matter. He would be addressed as his titles by everyone anyway. But it was much more intimate when there was a personal name that could be used, in her estimation, for those particularly intimate friends or family members. But this was one more area in which she was an oddling, she could see. Perhaps returning to the continent or finding some other destination would be the best thing for her after all. A quick glance over her shoulder showed that Peggy had disappeared once more. The search for another cousin would have to commence immediately. Connie managed not to sigh audibly.

Thankfully, the conversation had resumed swirling around her and no one seemed particularly concerned with her ridiculous question nor her ensuing preoccupation. Constance continued fumbling with her hostess' string.

"Don't let it bother you," Lady Adelaide whispered in a barely audible breath. "Until you have a child of your own on the way, you don't give these sorts of topics the first thought."

Connie smiled at the kind woman. She hadn't expected the offer of friendship, but she appreciated it immensely.

"How are you finding life at Everleigh?" Constance asked the rather broad question, wondering how the lady would answer it and hoping the other women didn't consider it rude that they start their own, private conversation.

"Complicated," the viscountess answered with a light laugh. "But that's part of what I love about it," she added. "We might have much in common. I just solved my situation more conventionally than you did."

Connie again wanted to stare at the viscountess. She wished they were alone so she could hurl all her questions at the other woman. But she managed to bite her tongue and keep them to herself. But they must have written themselves upon her face despite her best intentions.

"Shall we stroll in the gardens after this?" Lady Adelaide asked, still keeping her voice low, the invitation intended for Connie alone. Not used to such friendly gestures, Constance's heart swelled. It was an odd sensation. She hoped she wasn't coming down with something. She had already questioned her own health multiple times in recent days. She would have thought rusticating in the country would be good for her health, but she might be strange in that as in everything – different from everyone else as always.

She didn't bother answering, allowing her smile to be reply enough. Of course, she would stroll with her hostess.

It seemed to take half an eon for the needlework ladies to finish their projects or at least conclude they had been sufficiently virtuous for the day. Several decided they needed to lie down for a bit and the small party broke up. Some of the female guests had never joined and of course none of the gentlemen had done so either. Constance wondered where the others had gone off to. But she didn't suffer from feeling left out. Having a cozy visit with her hostess was going to more than make up for anything she might have missed elsewhere, she was certain.

"What do you think of Everleigh?" Lady Adelaide asked with gentle emphasis on the *you* in her question, as though she were immensely curious of Constance's answer.

"It's lovely but intimidating," Constance replied after a few sedate steps and many racing thoughts, causing her hostess to laugh.

"Yes, of course, but what do you really think of it? That's what everyone thinks. But you're not everyone."

"Why did you invite me here, my lady? Was my eccentricity to be your entertainment?" Constance tried to keep her voice steady and even, but the very thought of being a mockery made her heart want to stop cold in her chest.

"Oh, dear heavens, no, why would you even think that?"

Constance was somewhat mollified by the horror sounding in the viscountess' voice, but she couldn't help her suspicions.

"I haven't been invited to a house party in years," she began. "And we have never really been friends. I was surprised to receive your correspondence after you'd wed and then your invitation was an even bigger surprise. I hadn't thought we'd become such bosom friends through our letters."

Lady Adelaide laughed a little although she still appeared uncomfortable despite her step never faltering. "I'm sorry if I haven't made you comfortable here, Lady Constance. I have been curious about you, I will admit. I thought I wasn't so vulgar in my curiosity as to allow you to be uncomfortable as my guest, and I apologize if that isn't the case. But I had no intention of subjecting you to anything awkward or uncomfortable, I truly hoped to become friends. I was never completely conventional myself, so I thought we might have some things in common."

"You married into one of the wealthiest titles in the realm, my lady, and appear to be thriving in that position. I do not see how we have much in common."

Constance lifted her chin as her hostess stared at her. "You are far from an impoverished commoner, my dear," Lady Adelaide finally said in a low, wry tone. "But I was thinking more along the lines of our thought processes or opinions, rather than our circumstances. Perhaps I was wrong. But whether we are similar or not, I had hoped you would enjoy a sojourn in the country and I could enjoy your company. If that is not the case, please do not feel obliged to stay even though you accepted the invitation."

Now Constance felt small and petty. She should have remained delighted with the other woman's attention and interest rather than become suspicious of it. In her own defence, though, there had been times that she had found herself as a guest for various events where she was viewed as a curiosity rather than a guest of equal standing as the others. She hadn't conjured the idea.

"What do I think of Everleigh?" Constance turned the subject back to the viscountess' original question. "I think it is grand and you ought to have at least ten children to make its size feel appreciated."

Lady Adelaide laughed again but Constance was relieved to hear that it sounded genuine this time. "There are an inordinate number of rooms, aren't there? But ten children might be a little excessive, even for Everleigh. We cannot use the royal suite for anything so pedestrian as housing our children."

Connie laughed. “That suite is magnificent, but it does take up rather a great deal of space. Has His Highness ever visited?"

"The Prince of Wales has, from what I understand. Also, the King long ago. Adelaide just barely remembers it.”

“It does seem redundant to have an entire suite kept for a visit that might never happen.”

“It does, you are quite right. But what can you do?” Lady Adelaide laughed. “My ancestors never had such high aspirations so we had no such suite in my home. Did yours?”

“No, I cannot imagine there are so many out there.”

“Actually, I would expect there are. It seems to have been a condition upon which permission to build was granted, at least for a time.”

“It’s hard to imagine the Duke of Carlisle asking anyone’s permission, even the king.”

Lady Adelaide laughed. “You’re right. I would imagine he inherited that attitude along with his wealth from the previous generations of Carlisle. But I suppose, back then, when many of these beautiful, grand houses were built, it was an honor and a privilege, as well as a duty to house your sovereign monarch.”

“Of course,” Constance agreed immediately. “It probably still is,” she added, “so you ought to prepare your mind for the possibility.”

Lady Adelaide appeared suitably horrified for a brief moment before she covered it up with more laughter.

“Now, tell me truthfully, my lady, do you love wandering about or do you just do it to be interesting?”

Constance blinked at the sudden question. She tried to laugh it off but it was a very pointed, and somewhat insulting, question. How rude would it be for her to point out her hostess' rudeness? Since they were alone, she supposed it needn't become a scandal.

"Are you being intentionally provoking, Lady Adelaide?" she finally managed to ask with a reasonably even voice.

"Oh dear, was my question rude? I suppose it was. I do apologize. I didn't mean it as such. I was just so anxious to ask but didn't plan out the best way of doing so. Do say I haven't offended you unforgivably."

"Not unforgivably, no," Connie answered with a light laugh.

"I suppose I ought to explain what I meant by my poorly worded question," Lady Adelaide said with a sigh. "I often think it must be so lovely to not be so rooted in place. Being landed, as my husband's family is, does keep one in place more than some might like. I have thought of you on your rambles and felt a twinge of jealousy from time to time. But then I walk in the portrait gallery and listen to the stories of previous generations and I'm rather proud to be trying to carry on what they began. So, I would imagine there are blessings and benefits to every situation. Even yours. I was wondering if you've ever thought about changing your mind."

"And doing what, might I ask, my lady? Buy a cottage by the sea and breed cats?" Connie asked the question flippantly even though it was something she had begun to consider.

Lady Adelaide laughed loudly over that question, but then sobered. "And why not? If you were able to successfully traipse about the continent, I don't see why you couldn't make a success of that as well, if it were something you wanted."

"But that's just it, I don't. Want it, that is. I do enjoy my travels. It is true that it becomes lonely at times. But

I would imagine the cottage by the sea might be even more so." She couldn't have even explained why she was arguing. Somehow, she just couldn't yet admit aloud to the secret wish.

"Well, there are usually neighbours," the viscountess replied tentatively.

"So the same with travelling," Constance countered.

"Well, that's good then." Lady Adelaide surprised Constance with her sudden about face. "I just wanted to ensure you were still happy with your choice. If you weren't I would put my thoughts toward helping you."

Constance laughed lightly. "What do you think you could do to change my circumstances if you found I wasn't as happy with my situation as I had wished for?"

"Why find you a suitable husband, of course."

"Do you truly consider a husband to be the solution to all of life's woes? That's putting rather too much pressure on a poor man, isn't it?"

"For the right one it wouldn't be too much pressure," Lady Adelaide insisted.

"Perhaps," Constance allowed, "but I believe I ought to be able to find my happiness within myself and solve my own problems. If I then choose to wed with someone, that would be a happy addition, not the solution." They strolled in silence for a moment before Connie turned to her hostess with a frown. "If this is your view, what sort of dilemma were you in that your husband saved you from?"

"I was trouble," Lady Adelaide replied immediately. "I was always sticking my nose in the wrong situations. Out of boredom, I suppose. But falling in love with Adelaide provided me all the action I was craving."

Constance smiled over the woman's gleeful tone. The way she said it, marriage sounded delightful. But Connie's sisters seemed miserable, and their lives were drudgeries despite the supposed life of luxury one of her sister's had married into. It all just went to prove that nothing was a guarantee.

"Are you expecting any more guests to arrive?" Connie asked, to turn the subject and prolong the conversation.

"Yes, I am, a few more. Mr. Alcott wasn't the last straggler to arrive." Connie fought back heat that wished to flood her cheeks over the other woman's pointed words.

Chapter Six

After his first full day at Everleigh, Florent was confused. The house party was pleasant, although he found it odd that the gentlemen were so divided in their attentions. The married, older gentlemen who appeared to be the fathers of debutantes were anxious to be away from the women, interested in whatever sorts of sport Everleigh might have to offer. On the other hand, the single gentlemen seemed preoccupied with the women. Understandable, Flor allowed, but still, it resulted in an odd situation to find himself in. He was an eligible, single gentleman. He was a nobleman but not a peer. Not yet, anyway. He was heir to his father's viscountcy so while he was only currently Mr. Alcott, he would one day, hopefully not too soon, be Viscount Alcott with all the responsibilities and privileges that would entail. In the meantime, he worked very hard to increase what he was to inherit for his own benefit and for the rest of his family, at least his remaining sister.

But no one seemed to appreciate that fact. At least not in a manner that he could accept. Of course, most probably weren't aware and perhaps even thought him odd for his preoccupation with his father's estate, but when he had learned how dire the situation was, he couldn't just gad about and ignore it. He'd had all his younger siblings to think about besides his eventual inheritance.

Now, though, Alcott was on steady standing, thriving even. It was time to consider his options. And he had one more responsibility toward Alcott. He would need to produce heirs to take his own place when the time came. A shudder shivered through him. It really was an odd situation, always contemplating someone's death. His father's, his own. All for a chunk of land his ancestors had claimed.

That was the way of things. But for the first time in his adult life, Florent Alcott was actually in the strange situation of being wealthy and not too terribly busy. It was likely that for some this wasn't a strange situation. It was possible some of his peers' ancestors had not abused their estates and left it impoverished. Or even more likely, his peers might not find out until they actually inherit.

Florent was grateful his father hadn't kept it from him, even though it curtailed the carefree carousing he might have otherwise engaged in. The sort of thing his brothers enjoyed but he had never had the freedom for. But Florent couldn't regret the responsibilities he had taken on so young. He knew no different, so there was nothing to lament.

But he didn't really know how to socialize.

Take the young women at this house party for example. What was he supposed to talk to them about? Florent strongly suspected they wouldn't much care to know about the foaling taking place at Alcott this year, aside from perhaps to admire the baby horses when they were safely arrived, cleaned up, and presentable. They wouldn't want to hear about how he had agonized over the bloodlines and then worried about the timing of the births and whether or not the mares were eating enough.

"Shall we go shooting, Mr. Alcott?" Lord Bathurst called to him, and Florent tried to put his concerns behind him. As his mother had reasonably pointed out, they were well staffed with knowledgeable grooms. He really ought to leave the matter with them. But Florent had built up the entire herd of animals who were now at home on their extensive lands. He took the matter very seriously.

Smoothing a pleasant expression over his face, Florent smiled at the baron who had thus hailed him. "I'd be delighted, thank you." It was really the only acceptable response. And perhaps he could learn a little bit about the man's daughter. Lady Isabelle seemed to be a pleasant young woman. She might make an excellent viscountess one day.

"Tell me about Alcott," the older man invited, or perhaps demanded was the better word as they walked toward the copse of trees well beyond the house.

Florent gritted his teeth. He had always been too busy for the social whirl of the Season, but he supposed as the heir to a now wealthy viscountcy, he would have to expect that he was considered an eligible bachelor. Of course he was, he scoffed at himself. He should have thought of that before attending this event. While he hoped to possibly find someone he could consider for himself, everyone else was doing the same thing for themselves or their family members. He silently exhaled his frustrations and wracked his brain for an appropriate response.

"Well, Alcott is just the next estate over, so the land is quite similar in makeup. We even work similar crops and flocks. Have you discussed Everleigh with the earl or Adelaide?"

"I have a little. But of course, since Adelaide is wed now, it's not as likely to become a matter of real interest to me, now, is it?"

Well, that wasn't beating about the bush, was it? Florent fought an inappropriate laugh. In his mind it was actually a fully appropriate time to laugh, but the gentleman was unlikely to view it as such.

He cleared his throat trying to think how best to answer the question.

"I'm trying my hand at cotton this year," he finally offered.

"Cotton? Isn't that a bit daft out here so near the straight?" It was at least an intelligent question, Florent comforted himself. And the man hadn't actually asked for a count of the coins in his coffers.

"We might get a touch too much rain, but we're also the warmest part of the country. Some are having success with it and with the import taxes so high right now, it's a profitable business if you can make it work, so we thought to try it."

"Interesting. I haven't been one to innovate much at Bathurst. But younger men these days are much more adventurous."

Florent stifled his laughter once more. He hadn't considered his crops an adventure but perhaps they were. Not the sort that Lady Constance enjoyed but an adventure nonetheless.

"How are the plants faring, then?" Bathurst demanded, seemingly unconcerned that his booming voice might scare away the birds they were purported to be hunting. Florent supposed the invitation to shoot was just a way of getting him alone for questioning. He was clearly not of a sufficiently devious mind to be able to recognize the signs.

"We had a decent crop this year. Well enough that we will try an extra field next year."

Bathurst nodded. “Smart not to go all in until you know. None of your other crops suffered from the changes?”

“Not in the least. In fact, I consider it always a good idea to have a diverse range of crops to prevent widespread problems. And we try to rotate the fields from year to year. I haven’t yet tried allowing many fields to lie fallow. But so far, I haven’t found I’ve needed to consider it.”

“So you’re doing well for yourself it would seem.” The older man couched his words as a compliment, but Florent could almost see the older gentleman estimating his worth down to the nearest farthing. It was laughable on the one hand, but it also had the result of making him far less interested in pursuing Lady Isabelle. He knew it wasn’t the girl’s fault, but he couldn’t help feeling like an animal on the market. Shouldn’t the man be more interested in his character? Would that not be important for the man’s daughter? While it was responsible of Lord Bathurst to ensure any potential suitors were comfortable, Florent was of the opinion that a father should concern himself with how a man would treat his daughter, not how much he could spend on her.

Florent managed to get through the rest of the morning with the older gentleman by his side. He was able to ascertain that Bathurst was small for an earldom, and the man didn’t really know how to turn his fortunes around, merely following the same course that his father and grandfather had pursued. But he was a good-natured old fellow and it wasn’t the worst day of Florent’s life spent in the man’s company, so he was able to return to the house in relatively good spirits.

“Where have you been off to?” His sister greeted him upon his return, making Florent laugh.

“I would ask you the same question.”

"Really?" she demanded with a frown. "I've been asking everyone where you had gone off to. Only Lady Constance seemed to have any idea. She said she saw you going into the woods with Lord Bathurst and you both had guns. I had begun to worry."

Florent was fairly certain his sister was exaggerating facts in order to pull the wool over his eyes about something, and he wondered what it could possibly be. As the oldest sibling to her youngest born, he occasionally felt ancient next to her youthful exuberance even though only about ten years separated them. But she was much craftier than he could ever be and often turned his head with her stories. He had learned long ago to watch for them. This time was no exception. He narrowed his eyes at her.

"I find several things to dispute about your statement, little sister. What are you up to? As soon as you start making fanciful statements, I become suspicious. Two gentlemen going into the woods with guns usually means to hunt, not to shoot one another. Your worry, if was even in existence, was misplaced."

To Florent's surprise his sister just laughed and shrugged. But then, to his further surprise, Lady Constance came up and joined them, interrupting his tirade. Her colour was high as though she were embarrassed for cutting in but doing it anyway. His eyes narrowed. She was lovely but perhaps a little too bold. He was again reminded that he wouldn't mind befriending her but hoped his sister wouldn't do so.

"I'm not sure why you would be suspicious of your sister, and I apologize for eavesdropping but the two of you weren't exactly silent in your exchange. I really did see you going into the woods with Lord Bathurst and you both looked prepared for some shooting."

The presence of the beautiful woman made strange things happen to Florent. For the briefest moment he felt all thought flee his head, and he couldn't quite comprehend what she was saying as his heartbeat sped up and a shiver of nerves made its way through him. With a blink and a slight clearing of his throat, Florent was able to bring his mind back under his own control. With that, he frowned anew at Lady Constance. Why was she sticking her nose in his affairs?

"Thank you for the clarification, my lady," he finally said to her, even while frowning. She was distracting him. It wasn't really that his sister was referring to his going shooting that was the cause of his suspicions toward her, but he couldn't very well tell the other woman that.

"Has your traipsing through the forest made you thirsty, Mr. Alcott? There are refreshments being served in the front receiving room." She glanced down at his boots significantly, making heat climb up the back of Florent's neck. "If you'd like to change your footwear, Miss Alcott and I could wait here for you."

Florent's mouth opened and closed but no words were there for him to use. A quick glance at his sister told him she was highly entertained by his predicament and perhaps almost as confused by the other woman's interference.

Florent stared at his sister and Lady Constance for a brief moment, wondering if they were somehow in league together to confound him. He couldn't begin to fathom why that could be the case. He turned and hurried off without a word or a backward glance, only grateful that he didn't hear any feminine laughter following his retreating feet.

What was Daisy up to?

And why would Lady Constance interfere? Or was she interfering? Perhaps it just appeared that way due to his inordinate interest in her. Florent shook his head even as he pulled off his boots with the assistance of the boot jack by the door in the room he had been assigned. Making short work of righting his appearance, Florent wondered which would be the least cowardly action, staying in his room to avoid dealing with either woman or returning to the gathered guests and hoping it all became clear or his mother would deal with it.

It didn't mater which was cowardly or brave. Florent wasn't confident his mother would do anything about Daisy. Their mother used to be a formidable force but it would seem that successfully raising five children had worn her out and she no longer had the stamina for the sixth. It was possible she didn't wish to see the last of her brood married off, but Florent suspected the spirited Daisy was merely more than their mother could handle. It was one more duty he would have to perform for his family.

Florent had no idea how to act as matchmaker for his sister, but he would have to see for himself that she wed. It was likely their hostess had some ideas about matching his sister. From the little he had heard about social events of the Season, they were all for the purpose of pairing up potential couples, so it was likely that at least a modicum of thought had been put into who might match up with Daisy. Lady Adelaide was her friend, after all. It would behoove Florent to ask the gentlemen present a few uncomfortable questions such as Lord Bathurst had asked him. Although surely, he could figure out a more subtle way to do it.

As he combed his windblown hair back into order and had a servant tug a fresh coat onto his shoulders, Florent cudgeled his mind for ways to learn about a gentleman that didn't involve asking the actual worth of their estates. And would it be odd to ask another gentleman how he spent his spare time? Most likely. Perhaps he could begin with asking how much time they spent in Town and go from there. Surely that was the sort of thing people might discuss? Florent couldn't be sure since the only time he talked to people was for business purposes. He was greener than a debutante, he realized, and then tugged upon his cravat as another blush rode up his neck.

Regardless of his inexperience or his discomfort, he couldn't abdicate his responsibility toward his sister. Neither of their parents seemed to be concerning themselves, so, like everything else, it fell to him. He strode back down the grand staircase in search of the other guests.

Chapter Seven

Constance watched the door anxiously hoping Florent Alcott would appear. There was just something so steadying about the gentleman. Connie couldn't put her finger on it. Perhaps it was his size. He looked solid so it made an observer think he could be relied upon. In her experience, no one could be relied upon. And that was being proven to her in no uncertain terms at that very moment.

Henry Wagner had arrived.

How was Lady Adelaide even acquainted with the bounder? And why would she invite him as a guest into her home? A home with innocent young debutantes? Discomfort swirled in Connie's belly, but she tried to smooth out her features and appear unconcerned over the turn of events. And of course, keep from emptying the contents of her stomach into the nearest plant pot. That would surely not endear her to anyone.

Blessedly, with Daisy by her side, Wagner was keeping his distance. He was conquering the room while she stood helplessly by. Constance was going to keep Daisy glued to her as long as she possibly could. It no longer mattered that she had been hoping to assist the younger woman in whatever clandestine activities she was involved in. That no longer suited Connie's needs.

She hated to be selfish, but she was going to have to put her own needs first in this case.

Constance's first impulse when she discovered Wagner had been invited was to leave the premises immediately. But she couldn't do that to Peggy. Or rather she didn't want to, at least not yet. It would be completely craven on her part to flee without finding out what the weaselly man was up to, anyway. No one else would even think to consider that he was up to anything. Surely, he must be.

It could never be properly explained to Connie why the awful man was accepted everywhere. Why here he was even accepted as Viscountess Adelaide's guest! It was possible the lady was misguided enough to think she was doing Connie a favour. Constance was uncomfortably aware that it was thought the dreadful creature was courting her. As if she would allow that. But since he was thought to be an eligible *parti* she supposed others might think she would consider him. He was thought to be handsome and personable. And the depths of her own pockets meant she needn't consider his lack to be a matter of concern. In fact, there were many who would consider she owed it to humanity to bless some impoverished gentleman with her inheritance. Even if she were so foolish as to accept that sentiment as her own, she certainly wouldn't be doing so with Henry Wagner.

Constance didn't much care about the size of her coffers as long as she had enough to do what she wanted. She didn't have anything against economizing. She actually enjoyed the exercise of ensuring she didn't overpay. But that was a matter of principle. Just because she had lots didn't mean everyone was entitled to a portion of it. In line with that, she didn't consider herself obliged to find an impoverished gentleman to wed. In fact, she hoped she wouldn't do so because she would always wonder if it were she or her inheritance he was interested in. Besides, he wouldn't understand her life or her choices if he had never had wealth. She would remain an oddity for the rest of her days. And that would not do in the least. Especially not in her own future home.

But it wasn't the state of Henry Wagner's bank account that made him unacceptable to Constance. It was the way he treated people. To be sure, he knew how to say all the right things and he danced like a dream. His eyes gave him away, though. They sneered even when his lips were saying the correct and polite things that were expected of them.

Despite his seeming attention to whomever he was speaking to as he made his way around the room, Connie could feel his gaze flickering toward her from time to time. It was ratcheting her nerves higher each time, and she wondered if that was why he hadn't yet approached her, as though he knew he was driving her mad by drawing it out and prolonging the moment.

Constance had been introduced to Mr. Wagner in Italy. She had been younger and less experienced at the time and like everyone else, she thought him exceedingly handsome. But there was something about him that had immediately put her on guard. She had blamed herself at first. There must surely be something wrong with her to be feeling so completely opposed to everyone else's sentiments, she had thought.

But then she had been on the street one day and saw him kick a small child who was begging, and she had known that her instincts had been correct.

No one was overly enamoured with the beggars, but to kick one? Especially such a young one? That was unacceptable, and it had lifted Connie's blinders to the man's other undesirable qualities.

And that was before he had started trying to entrap her into marriage. She was grateful she had already become wary of him or he might have succeeded. As it was now, they seemed to regularly perform a dance where he would seek her out and she would evade him.

Henry Wagner was one of the reasons she had accepted the invitation to return to England for the house party. She had thought to have a break from the constant pressure of remaining one step ahead of the bounder.

And now here he was at Everleigh.

Constance had already been thinking she needed to contact her family to arrange a new companion. But she had been thinking to wait until she visited them in person and discussed the possibilities. Connie had seen enough of the world to know the signs. Lord Merton hadn't quite come up to scratch yet, but she had every confidence the nobleman was going to offer for her companion. It had been endearing and entertaining to witness when it was just going to cause an inconvenience. Things were different now.

Now, though, she knew she would have to write her mother right away. Connie couldn't be so cruel to Peggy as to pull her away from this opportunity at normalcy that she had always craved, but she had no intention of subjecting herself to the current circumstances any longer than necessary. Another companion was immediately necessary. Connie couldn't be left unprotected. And if she could have two companions, all the better. Connie couldn't be bothered by others thinking her even more eccentric than they already did.

If her mother could think of someone right away, she could send her to Everleigh to meet her and Connie would have an excuse to leave. It would take at least a day or two but it was something. Constance hated nothing more than inactivity.

Oh, she enjoyed sitting and reading as much as the next person. But that wasn't inactivity in her mind. What she loathed was dithering, she supposed. Worrying about a matter and doing nothing to solve it. That was anathema to her and not to be borne.

Her worries seemed to produce the result. Keeping Miss Alcott by her side was not the protection she had hoped.

"My dear lady, you seem to have grown even more beautiful in our brief absence."

It took every effort not to snatch her hand back from his as Mr. Wagner bowed and his lips hovered just above her wrist. Her gratitude knew few bounds when he didn't actually allow his lips to settle upon her skin.

"Mr. Wagner," she replied coolly. "What a surprise to find you here."

"A pleasant one, I do hope," he answered with a smile, hiding the sneer she could see in his eyes. *Why would he not quit pursuing her so?* "Pray introduce me to your friend, as we are not yet acquainted."

Connie didn't want to do it but there was little she could do to avoid the social nicety. To her relief though, after performing the introduction, Wagner didn't linger as he was hailed from across the room. Connie knew it as a temporary reprieve.

If Florent Alcott didn't enter the room in the next five minutes, Connie determined she would leave. She would go to her room and write her letter immediately. Perhaps she should do so whether the gentleman arrived or not. Constance really had no reason to believe she could rely upon him. Lingering in an uncomfortable situation expecting a near stranger to save her from it was actually quite ridiculous when considered objectively.

"His beauty doesn't reach his heart, does it?"

"I beg your pardon?" Constance stared at Miss Alcott at her side.

"I'm sorry, I thought out loud." The younger woman's blush nearly reached her hairline and Connie couldn't help smiling over that, but Daisy's discomfort quickly receded. "He looks a little like a rodent, don't you think? Like he's scheming how to steal the cheese."

Connie had to fight not to laugh right out loud in the Everleigh receiving room. To her knowledge, no one had ever seen through Henry Wagner before, except her. Connie's heart swelled. Perhaps she ought to stay on home soil more often. It seemed there were more like-minded people than she had ever realized.

"I wonder what he's conniving. It's surprising that Lady Adelaide would invite such a one to her party, isn't it?" Daisy was still musing over the man who was now across the room, much to Constance's delight.

"It might be my fault," Constance said quietly, which caused the young woman at her side to turn wide eyes filled with horror upon her.

"I am so sorry, I meant him no insult, perhaps it was a trick of the light." Daisy stammered and stumbled through an apology of sorts causing Constance to fight laughter once more.

"Not at all," Constance said, waving away Daisy's anxious words. "I am not offended in the least, and I also didn't word myself properly. It is thought that the man is courting me. I will not allow it, of course, but that is the rumour, no matter how hard I try to dismiss it. I am assuming that is why her ladyship invited the man."

"Ah, I see," Daisy said with a slight frown that indicated she didn't really. Constance didn't bother going into details.

"Ought I to ask Lord Adelaide to have him leave?" Daisy sounded a little nervous of the thought but willing to make the effort for Constance. Once more Constance was assured that coming home had been a good decision despite her current discomfort.

"No, no, that would probably cause more trouble than it was worth, although I certainly appreciate the offer. Thank you, Miss Alcott."

"Well surely, if we're getting personal, you ought to call me Daisy like the rest of my friends and family do."

Constance returned the other woman's grin. "Thank you, Daisy. And please, do call me Constance or Connie."

"But only while we're whispering, right?" Daisy asked with a giggle.

Connie smiled. "Shall we stroll outside? There was actually something I hoped to ask you."

"By all means, then," Daisy said. She gestured for Constance to precede her but then she glanced back anxiously at the other guests assembled.

"We can stroll later if you'd rather stay with the others," Constance quickly offered. Even as she had invited the girl, she had realized she couldn't ask her about her suspicions that she was getting up to something scandalous. If she was, what could Connie do other than scold her? And if she wasn't, it would only cause uncomfortable feelings between them. She would have to be creative to come up with something else to say if the girl accepted now.

"But you wanted to talk to me particularly, didn't you?"

Connie shrugged. "It was neither urgent nor of real note. It can wait." She tried not to frown when Daisy appeared relieved. What was the girl up to? Connie resolved to keep a sharper eye on the other woman. She quite liked her. Connie couldn't allow something to happen to her when it seemed she was the only one aware that there was even something out of the ordinary going on with her. Especially since Connie herself had aided in that lack of awareness. Guilt threatened to sweep her.

Just as Daisy was about to take her leave of Constance, her brother entered the room and relief swept through Connie instead. It didn't matter if the reaction was illogical. She would allow it because she hated the anxious feelings that had been churning within her since she'd been informed of Mr. Wagner's arrival. It oughtn't to be such a trial for her, but she couldn't help fretting over avoiding scandal. Especially one she didn't want to be a part of in the first place.

A sigh threatened to reveal the depths of her low feelings, but Connie managed to swallow it down and still keep a slight smile on her face. The depths of despair were not a usual location for her spirits, and Connie refused to allow them to take up residence there. Florent took his sister's place just as Daisy flitted across the room.

"Am I slightly more acceptable for Society now, my lady?" Florent asked sounding equal parts anxious and appalled to be even asking. Constance laughed lightly.

"Slightly, I suppose," she replied, a tease evident in her tone.

Florent bowed to her in acknowledgement and then turned to survey the room.

"I see the guest numbers have increased again."

"It would seem your neighbours are determined to fill their house to bursting." Constance kept her tone light, having no desire to reveal her thoughts on the subject. But Florent's gaze sharpened on her anyway.

"I think her ladyship is determined to be able to crow that she arranged the most matches of any hostess this

Season without even going to Town. There is no question that she is the competitive type."

"Has she always been a matchmaker?" Constance was genuinely curious. Lady Adelaide had debuted after she did, but they were slightly acquainted. Connie was more friends with Lady Adelaide's older sister, but Ellen had never mentioned her sister's tendency to matchmake. It was more the purview of older ladies or the mothers of daughters.

"I haven't known her long but according to her husband, it is a new pursuit."

Constance could hear laughter lurking in Mr. Alcott's voice and she warmed to him even more. Perhaps there was something in the ale at Everleigh. It was turning even sensible minded ladies into flirtatious ninnies. She ought to keep her distance. She ought to leave. But that would smack of cowardice, and no one could ever accurately accuse Constance of that.

"Are you well?" The soft question, in the low voice, just behind her ear sent a shiver down her arms and a warm furl of comfort and something else in her belly. It felt for a moment as though he had caressed her even though he kept an appropriate, polite distance from her.

"Why do you ask?" Her question was barely above a whisper. Constance didn't want anyone else to know there was even the slightest possibility that she was anything but perfect. But Florent seemed to have the uncanny ability to read her thoughts and intentions.

"I cannot say for certain, but it seems to me that you are uneasy. And I think it has to do with the new arrivals."

Being much younger than her siblings and not terribly close with them and then feeling so different than everyone else wherever she went, Constance had never been in the habit of unburdening herself upon anyone, let alone a handsome gentleman she had only become reacquainted with. Certainly, she would never do so in a crowded receiving room where anyone could overhear. But she had never been so tempted to do so as she was in that moment.

Shaking her head a little, she smiled at him to soften her rejection of his offer.

"I am perfectly fine, thank you so much for your concern."

He leaned in closer so that there was no possibility anyone could overhear.

"You are lying," he stated boldly but not unkindly. "But you can change your mind and talk to me if you ever wish to."

Constance blinked, hoping her feelings were not writing themselves upon her face. She didn't even know what she was feeling, so she most definitely didn't want anyone else to see her turmoil. From the warmth in his eyes, though, she was reasonably sure Florent could sense some of it.

Her smile felt tight as she turned away from him with a mumbled goodbye and barely a curtsy. She went in search of someone else, anyone else, to talk to. A frantic glance around the room indicated there was an empty spot on the settee next to Lady Bathurst. Constance hoped she wasn't taking anyone else's place but decided her own need in that moment was stronger.

"Hello, my lady," Constance greeted simply as she sat down. "I do hope it's all right for me to join you for a moment." She smiled gently and received very little reaction from the other woman. "The room has suddenly grown fuller, and I find I need a slight reprieve."

Lady Bathurst patted Connie's hand. "That's perfectly fine, dear. It happens to all of us eventually."

Connie bit the side of her tongue to prevent it from expressing her thoughts. Was the woman equating them? As though to imply that Constance was of an age with the matron? Her stomach curdled slightly at the thought, but there was no counter argument she could possibly make. Her smile was weak, but she offered it anyway.

Despite Lady Bathurst's questionable welcome and acceptance of her, Constance was glad she had taken the chance to sit down. She could feel Mr. Wagner's gaze fixed upon her once more, but she knew her presence next to the older woman would keep the bounder at bay for the time being. She would have to speak with him again eventually if they were to be fellow guests, but for now she would take the reprieve no matter how craven she might consider it to be.

Conversation swirled around her, but her years of practice participating in the social niceties kept her in good stead. Connie didn't have to pay the least bit of attention to what was being said. She knew exactly how to respond in all the appropriate places. It allowed her mind to race with the possibilities.

Was Henry Wagner present to continue his pursuit of her? In a certain way she ought to be flattered.

Perhaps it had nothing to do with her and she was being unforgivably vain.

Or he was up to no good as she always suspected, and she would have to do something about it because she was the only one who would possibly suspect him of anything. She valiantly ignored the fact that both Daisy and her brother had noticed at least something was amiss.

Connie ensured that her racing thoughts did not reflect themselves upon her features by keeping a small but pleasant smile pinned to her lips. She only hoped no one started talking about anything truly serious or saddening because then she would be completely inappropriate. But thus far, the position had allowed her to let her mind wander without fear of repercussions.

Why was Henry Wagner at Everleigh?

Really, until she asked him directly or Lady Adelaide, or both, there was no way for her to know. She couldn't possibly guess at the workings of the man's mind. Perhaps, unbeknownst to her, he was some long distant relative of Lady Adelaide or the Northcotts. They were certainly a large enough family. And everyone had unfortunate members on their family trees. Ones you were obliged to invite to your home upon occasion. She really shouldn't allow her overly active imagination to paint monsters in every closet. It was entirely possible that it was a purely innocent coincidence.

But Connie didn't believe in coincidences. And from what she had come to know about Mr. Wagner, there was never anything innocent about the man. She sighed.

Unfortunately, despite her advancing years, Lady Bathurst had nothing wrong with her hearing. Her sharp gaze settled upon Connie instantly.

"Are you finding the social interplay too tiring? There's nothing shameful in needing a nap," she reminded Connie kindly.

Connie hid her amusement as best she could and nodded to the woman. She was only trying to be kind after all.

"You could be right, my lady, I thank you for your concern."

Without bothering to try to explain herself, Connie left her place on the settee and took her leave of the room. While she didn't feel in the least bit tired, a little time alone would not go unappreciated.

Chapter Eight

Florent watched Lady Constance drift from the room. It was quite a fascinating feat. He had never noticed a person drift before. To his mind it seemed quite deliberate, as though she didn't want to be noticed or seen as leaving. Florent only witnessed it because he had been watching her attentively. He was trying not to. He had no interest in being accused of courting the woman. Not that there would be anything wrong with doing so nor would anyone try to stop him, but he felt an aversion to being pressured.

And there was the small fact that he needed to ensure his sister found a match. He couldn't consider Lady Constance to be a good influence upon Daisy, and that needed to be taken into consideration.

Perhaps it was because he did find her so very attractive that he was somehow fighting the impulse. Whatever the case, he had his eye on her and he knew she was uncomfortable and trying to hide it. He also knew she had exited the room with stealth. There was no other word for it. She had reminded him of a cat, to be frank. That image brought a smile to his face.

"What are you up to?" his sister asked him suspiciously, startling him.

Florent had been so busy thinking about Lady Constance that he hadn't even noticed Daisy sidling up to him. Another cat reference. Perhaps Florent was losing his mind. Being stuck at Alcott for his entire life had finally turned him into a simpleton just as he'd always feared. He was a crazy cat gentleman. What was he to do?

The droll thought kept him from snarling at his sister so he would have to be glad about that.

"I might very well ask you the same thing, Miss Alcott," Florent said with significant emphasis on the formality of her name. "I would have expected to see you right in the center of your dear friend's social event being held seemingly in your honour."

Florent watched his sister blush with chagrin but still lift her chin in defiance of his views. She was often such an independent little soul. She wasn't going to appreciate his admonishment, but Florent couldn't ignore her behaviour.

"I don't know what you're talking about, Flor," Daisy insisted. "I've been right in the center of it for days. You have just arrived. You haven't a basis for such a judgmental opinion."

Florent stared at his sister and wondered for a moment if his suspicions of her were misplaced but then there was a flicker at the back of her gaze as though she couldn't quite hold her nerves steady, and a grin bloomed on his face.

"You forget that I've known you longer than you've known yourself, little sister. I have been well aware of your tells, especially the ones on your face that you've almost grown able to hide, since you were able to speak. You've always been saying a different thing with your face and eyes than with your mouth. And right now, I know you're trying to hide something from me. And I don't like it in the least. Are you courting scandal for some reason? Are you resisting the one thing you claim to wish for?"

He watched his sister stare at him with her mouth slightly ajar as though she wished to say something but hadn't a clue what that was. Then she laughed. It was such a sound of joy that for a moment it reached his heart, and he was glad for her even if he didn't understand her.

Florent wanted his sister to be happy. This sister in particular. He was the closest with the youngest child in the family. It had seemed to Florent that his parents had left her to him to care for. He had missed her immensely when he had been sent to school, but they had always picked up where they'd left off whenever he'd returned home. And then, of course, she'd learned to write and had nearly bankrupted the estate with the amount of paper she'd used sending him lengthy tomes filled with all her childish thoughts and the goings on at home.

He probably had never expressed to her how much those letters had meant to him even as a boy. Of course, things had changed when he'd become so preoccupied with the estate. He only had himself to blame. Wanting to protect Daisy from the reality of their situation had put a wedge between them. But he couldn't allow that to stop him now.

Because he loved her so much, he couldn't allow her to get herself into a bind.

"Why won't you tell me what you've been doing, if it isn't anything questionable?"

"Do you really want to hear about the picnics and the strolls to the village and such things that you've missed when you were dealing with the livestock at home?"

When she put it like that Florent almost questioned his own judgment for the briefest moment. Which was exactly her intention, the little imp. He saw it in the crinkle in the corners of her eyes that she just couldn't hide from him.

"I would really like to hear all of that. It will help me feel like I haven't missed out."

A twinge of guilt swept through him when his tender-hearted sister appeared suddenly dismayed. No longer defiant, she stepped closer, tucking her small hand into his elbow, she demonstrated her affection easily.

"I'm so sorry, Flor, I shouldn't be grumbling at you. Of course, I'll tell you everything. Amelia has been a talented hostess, and everyone has been having a lovely time. But you haven't really missed out because it took a few days for everyone to arrive. Even today, you aren't the only arrival. That gentleman over there named Henry Wagner, he just arrived today, too. So don't feel as though you've missed out. Or at least don't feel that you've lacked because even though it has all been quite lovely, it hasn't been extraordinary, so I am quite convinced that the best is yet to come."

Florent had almost missed the change in his sister's inflection when she mentioned the other gentleman who'd arrived, as he had his own reaction to that man's presence. As far as Florent could tell, he didn't know the man, but he instinctively had a guarded reaction to him. And he suspected Daisy did, too.

"Why don't you like him?" he had lowered his head as well as his voice in order to ask his sister the question as privately as possible in the room full of people.

Daisy stared at him and briefly sputtered for a moment before a grin broke over her active features. "You do know me well, don't you, big brother?" She allowed her gaze to sweep the room before returning it to her brother's face. She lifted one shoulder in a gesture that looked slightly helpless. "I cannot truly say why I don't, as I have just barely been introduced to him, but he gives me a creepy feeling as though he is something different underneath his seemingly handsome exterior. Which is why I say seemingly handsome, because for me he doesn't look handsome due to that feeling I get, but I suspect others might consider his appearance appealing."

"I think it's the eyes," Florent agreed with a smile. "They are definitely shifty."

Daisy laughed. "And small. Almost beady. Like those of a rat or some other sneaky rodent."

"Exactly," Florent agreed immediately, relieved to be restored to his usual comfortable relationship with his sister. "Now carry on with your expository of all the good things you've been doing."

Daisy's delightful laugh sounded, bringing the attention of some in the room to rest upon them momentarily, but then everyone else resumed their own conversations, and Daisy began her list.

Florent only half listened. He wasn't in fact terribly interested in the details of what he had missed, but he had sensed something in his sister's demeanor when he'd first seen her. That and the fact that she hadn't been present when he'd arrived had both conspired to raise the hackles of his suspicions. As he had told her, he'd known her longer than she'd known herself. As the oldest sibling to her youngest, he'd been a boy of ten when she'd been born. Most would expect that a ten-year-old boy would take no interest in a newborn girl child, but Florent had taken one look at her and his heart had been seized. As the oldest, he had always felt all his siblings were his responsibility, but this youngest one all the more so.

They weren't inseparable by any means. They had their squabbles like all siblings did. And he had, of course, gone off to school as was expected of the Alcott heir. But he had taken note of all her traits, and he often felt that he knew her best. She had been the one to pour out her heart to him as a child and even as she'd grown older. It was only in recent years, when he'd become too tied up with estate business and she'd become more introspective as her debut came and went without a match, that she didn't confide her every thought to him. And it made him uneasy. He knew it would happen eventually, that she would wed and transfer her confiding love to someone else. But it hadn't happened yet, and he worried for her. When Daisy kept things to herself, she tended to land herself in trouble.

So he listened for her tones, waiting to note where there were missing bits. And there were definitely things being left out in her narrative. But he didn't really suspect she was truly courting scandal. His darling sister was still too conventional, despite the adventurous side that she tried to keep hidden. Unlike Lady Constance.

Florent almost clicked his tongue in dismay but caught himself before giving that telltale sign. He didn't want Daisy examining him as he was doing to her. It was obvious she was preoccupied with something, or she would have already noticed that his mind was only partially engaged. But the rest of his thoughts had followed Constance Moreland from the room. He tried to drag them back to his concerns about his sister. What if she was going to want to follow in Lady Constance's footsteps and become an eccentric?

For all his love of his little sister, he didn't think she had the fortitude to carry it off. Florent was surprised that Lady Constance had that fortitude. It couldn't be easy always being different from everyone else, especially for a woman. It might actually take concerted effort to do so, he would imagine. Again, his curiosity was engaged. And again, he fought a growl. His sister obviously needed him, but his thoughts were entangled with a different female.

Daisy prattled on about picnics and archery and visits to the village for a few moments, and Florent tried to be interested, he truly did. Perhaps if his thoughts weren't so divided between the present and his responsibilities still at home, never mind the lovely young woman who had captured a large part of his brain as soon as he had encountered her, he might have found Daisy's recitation interesting. He loved his sister and enjoyed her turn of phrase whenever she was describing something to him. But this time he just couldn't quite do it. Until she started asking him about smuggling in the area.

"Have you ever heard of anyone using the river behind Alcott and Everleigh for smuggling?"

Florent was even more relieved that they had strolled away from the others. "Smuggling? What would make you ask about that?"

Daisy's shrug was almost completely innocent, but Florent had managed to bring all his faculties back into alignment, and he knew for certain that something wasn't quite right with his sister. "I'm curious, is all. You know me, always sticking my nose into things."

"That's an odd thing for a lady to stick her nose into, isn't it?"

Daisy shrugged again but this time Florent actually believed it, and he fought a smile. Of course, his sister wouldn't concern herself if something was ladylike or not. For such a feminine creature, she didn't put much effort into it.

"I know we're rather far from where someone would expect smugglers to be, but after a walk on the moors, I was thinking it was actually a rather perfect location for such an activity. Being far from the usual place would probably provide some protection from detection."

"And so you thought to take up a career in criminology?" Florent frowned, wondering where his sister was going with her tale.

She shrugged once more and Florent was beginning to detest her nonchalance.

"I thought to write about it and so I was giving the matter some thought."

Flor wasn't sure if he believed that explanation, but his sister was known for spinning a good story from time to time. It was more plausible than her taking up the task of illegal importation, that was certain. But Florent still wasn't convinced that her question was as innocent as that.

"So you haven't heard of smuggling in these parts?" Daisy persisted. "What would you do if you did hear?"

"I'd have to look into the matter," Florent said. "And I'd be highly curious how the person I heard it from knew of the matter."

Daisy's mouth widened into a grin. "Would you suspect them?" Her eyes danced with delight at the prospect. "Do you think I might make a good smuggler?"

Florent laughed. "I think you might possibly be devious enough."

"Do you really?" Florent didn't appreciate how delighted she seemed by the thought. "I wouldn't have thought so."

"Does that disappoint you? Most wouldn't want to be thought devious."

She hummed in response, deep in thought. "I suppose I wouldn't want to be thought to be currently devious, as in I wouldn't want you to think I was lying to you. But I would like to be thought intelligent enough to be devious."

"I certainly think you are."

"Why Florent, that is such a sweet thing to say."

"You are quite the strange little thing today, my dear."

"Perhaps the fresh air has addled me."

"It's more likely that the not so fresh air of being in Town these past weeks is what has done it."

Daisy grinned again, not in the least bothered by his ribbing.

"Are things truly set to rights at home, Florent?" she asked next, quietly searching his face.

"Nothing to worry you in the least."

"That was not the question, Flor, and well you know it."

"See what I mean about being intelligent enough for deviousness."

Daisy's laugh tinkled forth, but she continued to watch him from the side of her eyes with an elevated eyebrow even as she strolled at his side.

Florent sighed. "As right as they can be for the time being. Thank you for asking, Daisy. There's nothing for you to be concerned about. I'm sorry that I wasn't able to come up to Town with you. But perhaps after this party I can come."

Daisy waved her hand in an all-encompassing gesture. "Perhaps it shan't be needed. Amelia has put a great deal of thought into matching me up to her specifications."

Florent grinned. "I can't tell how you feel about that from your varying tones. I'd suspect a mixture of feelings."

"Quite a smorgasbord of emotions, to be sure," Daisy agreed promptly. "Mostly appreciation, though, so have no fear. I love that she made this effort to help me. She was quite right that a house party is a far better means of getting to know someone than a crowded ball or rout."

"And did she do a good job of selecting candidates?"

"Exceptional."

"Have you chosen then?"

Daisy shrugged again. "Not yet," she said with a sigh. "Perhaps you could do it for me."

Florent laughed, thinking she was jesting, but she didn't laugh with him. Suddenly more concerned, Florent patted his sister's hand where it was still safely tucked into his elbow. He could now understand his mother's reluctance to arrange Daisy's match. He wanted to bundle her into the carriage and keep her safely at home.

"You really ought to have a preference, I would think," Florent said firmly to his sister before they were both distracted by new arrivals into the room.

Florent watched as Daisy smiled her appreciation to him before she untucked her hand from his arm and joined her friends. Momentarily he felt bereft before he turned his own attention to enjoying the rare experience of being entertained.

Chapter Nine

What was Henry Wagner doing here?

Constance paced her room in her stockinged feet, not wanting anyone to take note of her restlessness. The sound of her shoes tapping on the hardwood floor would give her away in a minute if anyone were to note it. And she had claimed the need to rest. Amusement flitted through her. She was doing the exact opposite of resting, to be sure.

What could he be up to?

Who could she trust with her concerns?

Constance didn't know or trust anyone at the gathering. Instinctively she felt as though she could trust Mr. Florent Alcott with her knowledge and even her life, but that was being more melodramatic than the situation called for. While her independence might be at stake if Wagner were to do as he wished and compromised her into being able to marry her wealth, she didn't think he would actually harm her, not beyond what was necessary to do the compromising, anyway.

Connie sighed.

She would have to pull Peggy away from whatever pursuits she was involved in. Connie knew her dear friend and companion was quietly resuming an old courtship that had gone wrong years ago. She didn't have all the details and she hesitated to interfere, but Peggy was needed here at the moment. Connie was singularly averse to being compromised.

Connie would admit to a certain curiosity about the process of being compromised. When she had her Season, she had a friend or two who had been found in the embrace of the gentleman they were interested in, which had resulted in a hasty betrothal. But that was not the sort of thing she feared from Wagner. Or perhaps it was.

She did not want to find herself forced into his company for the rest of her days. And while she might be curious about the embraces her friends had seemed to enjoy, she had absolutely no desire to share such intimacies with Mr. Henry Wagner. Nor did she wish to be forced into anything with him, let alone a life-long attachment. She was particularly opposed to the force element of being compromised, she supposed. The removal of her options.

She would never forgive a man who would do that to her. She really didn't care if he felt he was entitled. He was no relation to her. How could he actually think he was entitled to her inheritance? It was her own dear grandmother who had bequeathed her the money that was in this moment causing her to quake in her chamber.

Another shiver ran through her as she remembered the last time she had a run-in with Mr. Wagner. It had been at a villa in Hannover. Connie had blocked much of the experience from her mind and in her distress of that moment she couldn't even remember the name of her host. What she couldn't forget was the feel of Wagner's hot breath as he tried to force a kiss upon her. He hadn't accounted for her strength, both physical and of character, and so wasn't expecting the hard shove with which she freed herself from his arms. Just in time to not be found in his arms when someone he had evidently arranged to show up at the opportune time had come along. If she hadn't been so furious and humiliated, she might have been amused by the expression of disappointment upon both gentlemen's faces. Clearly, they had an agreement. She wondered how much Wagner had offered the other man for his role.

How did Wagner get invited to Everleigh?

That was really the question Constance was bothered by. On the continent, it had been one thing. The entire community of foreigners tended to accept one another quite freely and would be invited to all manner of entertainments on the merest acquaintance. But an English house party? At an Earl's country seat? That would take someone actually vouching for you if you weren't known to the host or hostess personally. This was much more serious.

Who had vouched for Henry Wagner?

Constance's pacing was getting her nowhere closer to an answer. She finally strode to the bell pull and yanked on the one that would summon her maid. She was the only one she could trust. Any one of the Everleigh servants could have been bribed. And Constance needed Peggy to attend her immediately. Her maid would have to find her and bring her to Connie's room. Connie didn't feel safe enough to find her herself. She didn't care if that sounded deranged even in her own mind. Her feelings were valid and based on experience.

Her pacing increased as she waited impatiently for the maid's return with her companion. Constance finally forced herself to settle into a chair next to the locked door. She was going to make herself sick or wear a rut in the floor if she didn't stop her restlessness.

Finally, the scratch on the door sounded her companion's arrival but still Connie didn't feel safe.

"Who is it?" she called, not unlatching the door until she heard Peggy's familiar laugh.

"Who do you think it is?" came the sarcastic reply.

With a huff, Connie opened to her companion and her maid.

"Quickly, come in," she said with an anxious glance down the hall.

"What has happened?" Peggy asked with a frown. "I thought your maid was being dramatic when she summoned me in what appeared to be a panic, but I can see from your hectic countenance there was cause for her concern. Are you ill?"

Without preamble Connie blurted out: "Henry Wagner is here."

"Wagner?" Peggy repeated as though dumbfounded. "How could he have finagled an invitation to such an exclusive house party?"

"Perhaps it's not as exclusive as we'd thought."

"Well, it certainly isn't peopled with a crush of guests like most balls you would attend in Town."

"True, but he's here, so it matters little. He must have been invited or he'd have been shown the door."

Peggy stared at her friend and employer. "You want to leave, don't you?"

"I am uncertain. Or rather, I am divided on the matter. Yes, a good part of me does want to run far from here, although another part of me questions what good that would do. If he could impose upon us here, he can do so anywhere, it would seem. And the rest of me is starting to have a good time here and doesn't wish to leave yet, despite the threat. Besides, I hate the thought of running craven."

Peggy nodded with understanding. "So, you need me to remain by your side no matter the circumstances, right? To lend you countenance and ensure the bounder cannot force you into matrimony."

"I know it's an imposition, Peggy, and I apologize, but there's nought else I can do. Or rather, perhaps I can ask, would you rather leave here than be glued to my side?"

Peggy grinned and reached for her friend's hand. "Constance Moreland, you are not a burden, and you needn't apologize for asking me to do what you pay me to do. Of course, I will stick with you."

Connie searched her companion's face. "I had the impression you were enjoying the freer circumstances to pursue an opportunity for yourself."

Peggy lifted one shoulder as though to dismiss Connie's words even as a blush stole over her cheekbones. "If the opportunity is right, it shan't disappear."

Connie's lips stretched into a ghost of a smile. She wasn't sure if she was going to be able to stomach being such a close witness to her friend's courtship, but it was that or leave. And she really did want to allow Peggy the opportunity to find her own life, even if it would by force rearrange Connie's situation. Even if Peggy were to become affianced, she could still provide the protection Connie would need until another companion could be arranged.

With a sigh, Constance wondered why she was trying so hard. Perhaps she should just find a suitable husband and be done with it. At least if she chose for herself, she wouldn't be forced or tricked into an even less welcome arrangement.

She couldn't allow herself to be tied for life to someone who would ensnare her. It would be far different if the bounder professed feelings for her. That would perhaps even carry a hint of romance that could reconcile her to her fate. But no, the sneaky cretin just followed her around coveting her wealth and somehow, he had developed a conviction that he was entitled to it. Perhaps he was deranged. All the more reason to keep him at arm's length.

"Still, Peg, I'm sorry. I was hoping this week we could each have the freedom of true independence."

"Well, my dear, that was a daft wish, wasn't it? We're women of the upper echelons. Despite your pursuit of independence, it's merely a façade. You cannot actually claim independence when you need to hire someone to accompany you."

Constance knew her friend wasn't being mean or cruel. It was truth she was speaking. But still, it felt a little like she had been stabbed in the heart. The shine was definitely wearing off the glow of her life of travel. But she refused to be saddled with such a specimen as Henry Wagner, no matter the cost.

"Tell me about his lordship," she invited Peggy, longing for a distraction.

"Now?" Peggy questioned. "Don't you need a nap or a change of attire or something? Isn't that why you summoned me?"

"I summoned you because I cannot be alone without a peer to protect my fragile situation," Constance reminded her with an edge to her voice. "I claimed to need a rest, but you know I slept reasonably well while travelling. I just needed to get away from that room for a moment. It was a sense of panic, to be honest."

Now Peggy truly appeared concerned. "You never panic," she said with her eyes wide and staring.

"I've never been followed about with quite this much determination," Connie answered, gritting her teeth.

"And finding him here, where I had every reason to think I would be completely safe for at least a se'en-night, was disheartening."

"Of course, it was, you poor dear. Tell me, what can I do?"

"Distract me for a moment so I can settle and so I'm not bored while we sit here for a few minutes in support of my claim to need a moment. I really would love to hear about what you have going on."

Peggy blushed. "I don't have anything going on as you rather crassly put it, my lady."

Connie laughed. "Don't get all starchy with me. Are we not friends? Please, my mind is scattered. I beg of you, tell me. I promise to be happy for you. But I do want to know. Truly. Not just as a distraction."

Peggy sat beside her mistress on the bed and clasped her hand for a moment. "I know, my dear, and I'm sorry for hesitating. I'm just afraid that it's too nebulous. It'll be like trying to catch mist if I talk about it too much right now. But you're right. We are friends. I will tell you what I can. But truly, there's not really anything to tell you right now."

Connie grinned. "There's enough to tell if you have that many fanciful words already."

Peggy giggled. She actually giggled. Connie wouldn't have thought her rather serious companion had such a sound within her.

"You are correct, I suppose. Lord Merton is enough of a gentleman that he wouldn't spend that much time talking to me if he weren't at least a little serious about it, wouldn't you say? Although, to be honest, he sort of courted me years ago, and nothing came of it then, either."

Connie bit her lip. So, it was true. Lord Merton. She had been under the impression that gentleman was courting the frequently disappearing Miss Alcott. Connie hadn't paid enough attention to whom Peggy had been spending time with. Did that make her a terrible person? She rather suspected it did. She wasn't sure if she ought to warn the other woman against him or not. It might appear churlish if she did, but would it be better to allow Peggy to learn the more painful way?

"I've always heard of him as being a perfect gentleman," Connie finally answered. "But he would have been very young for courtship if he tried courting you years ago."

Peggy grinned first but then frowned. "Why did you hesitate to answer at first? Do you know something about him that I ought to be aware of?"

Connie didn't know whether she ought to say something but couldn't avoid it now. "I thought he had been invited to court Miss Alcott. I would hate for you to be led along and hurt."

"Well, I can assure you my emotions are not yet that engaged. But I also think the gentleman was invited to find a match, not a specific one. I have the impression Lady Adelaide will be most pleased by any matches she can claim ownership of; she doesn't really mind who matches with who."

"Do you think she's that indiscriminate?"

"I wouldn't have thought so until I heard Mr. Wagner was present, to be honest. I had thought she had been highly selective and that was why she didn't much care who matched with whom."

"I suppose you are correct. Although, I do think she is particular friends with Miss Alcott."

Peggy shrugged and grinned. "Miss Alcott can only wed with one."

Connie laughed. "That is a true fact. But I am still left wondering why you have not started listing his many fine, sterling qualities."

Peggy giggled again, much to Constance's delight. "He is a fine, steady gentleman, but I fear you would find him boring, my lady."

Connie blinked. "Am I such a stickler, then?"

"Not overly so, but your sense of adventure is far more developed than is his."

"I suppose we could stipulate that mine is more developed than most people's."

"True enough," Peggy agreed immediately with another happy grin. Connie was more determined than ever that her friend find the life she most wanted. "He is a trifle fastidious. There was some complaining about the state of the roads. But once he got past that, he has plenty of interesting conversation. We share the same taste in books and food, and his estate isn't terribly far from your family."

"Why should that be a consideration? I am not thinking of him."

Peggy laughed again but this time it was a little forced. "No, you are not. But your family has become my family, have they not?"

Contrite, Connie squeezed her friend's hand. "Of course, they have. In fact, as a distant cousin, they have always been your family. You must forgive me. My brain has been addled."

Peggy laughed anew. "The solution is you will just have to get to know him for yourself. I am not doing a fine job of explaining him, I can tell. But he is quite lovely and exactly what I would seek if I were free to seek a husband."

"There is no encumbrance to your wedding, Peggy, surely you know that. I have loved having you as my companion these past years, but I know it is not where your heart is. I could not in good conscience drag you along with me if there was another situation for you. Please, don't give me a second thought." She laughed lightly and corrected herself. "Rather, of course you will give me a second thought, but please don't allow it to weigh with you. If you find this gentleman acceptable and he comes up to scratch, I will happily stand with you at your wedding before I drag some other hapless female off to travel the world."

Peggy appeared torn between being dubious and delighted. "But what will you do, truly? Won't you mind having to get comfortable with someone new?"

Connie put her arm around her companion. "It is a part of life. And if I cannot adjust to a new companion, then I'm not worthy of what Grandmother Asquith entrusted me with. Now, I *will* impose upon you to protect me from Wagner's wiles. But that is as far as I will go. You mustn't worry overmuch about my situation. It will work out."

"You could wed," Peggy suggested gently. "I saw you seemed quite content in Mr. Alcott's company."

"How did you have any time to note what I was up to? You seemed terribly occupied with your own concerns." Constance wasn't even going to countenance Peggy's statement with a more specific reply.

"I am fully capable of keeping my wits, surely you know that. Now tell me about Mr. Alcott. He has just yesterday arrived, so I haven't learned anything about him."

"Are you going to set your cap for him, too?"

Peggy suddenly appeared as though Connie had slapped her, and Constance was instantly contrite.

"My dear, I am so sorry. That was a jest that went beyond the bounds. Do forgive me. I am trying to adjust my thought pattern and haven't fully succeeded."

The two women sat in silence each with an arm around the other, offering comfort and companionship as they both sank into their own thoughts.

Peggy sighed. "I'm the one who's sorry, Connie. I knew what I was doing when I accepted your invitation to accompany you. I thought I would be content to travel the world at your side. I truly thought I would enjoy it immensely. And that isn't to say that I haven't enjoyed it. I have, as a matter of fact, even more than I would have expected. But I do long for a family and a home of my own. And if I can take this chance, I'm going to have to do so."

"Of course, you are. Has anything been said?"

"No, not yet. And perhaps it will all come to nought."

"Well then he would be a fool and unworthy of you," Connie returned immediately. "If Lord Merton doesn't come up to scratch and offer for you, we will find you someone else."

Peggy laughed. "Am I to be your project now, then?"

Connie smiled at the question but couldn't join her in laughter. There were too many concerns swirling in her head, but she was trying not to be selfish about it. Peggy needed to be provided for. Connie could see that clearly now. She would accept that her companions were to be temporary in the future as this was sure to happen again.

"Is there any possibility you might wish to settle down as well, my lady?" Peggy's question was hesitant as though she feared broaching the subject.

"Not likely, Miss Smith," Connie returned with a smile over her companion's return to being more formal. "You weren't mistaken, I do enjoy Mr. Alcott's company.

But can you really imagine my settling down to be a landowner's wife? Staying in one place for the rest of my days? The man doesn't even go up to Town."

"He would have to when he inherits, wouldn't he? To take his seat, I mean?"

Connie laughed. "You are truly conventional, aren't you?"

"There's no need to become insulting, my lady," Peggy countered with laughter, knowing full well her mistress meant her no insult but also understanding the noblewoman's view of conventionality. "But to answer your question, I can in fact see you settling down. I think you could do anything you set your mind and heart to. For now, that has been traveling around and seeing everything there is to see. In the future, it could very well be something else. There is no need to limit yourself, even in your own mind."

"Perhaps not, but marriage is terribly permanent. And would be limiting by its very definition."

"It would also avail you of other opportunities that might not be considered limits by many."

Again, Connie squeezed her friend with the arm that was around her but then she jumped up and resumed her pacing.

"This is all very well and good to be debating, but it doesn't change the current situation. Henry Wagner is at Everleigh, and I need to find out why. I am uncertain how to find out. I am open to your suggestions."

"Have one of your servants start inquiries. Is that not why you travel with such an entourage?"

Connie laughed. She had grown so used to the multiple servants she brought with her everywhere, she had nearly forgotten about them. "You are a genius, my dear." Having a course of action, however small, filled her with purpose.

Chapter Ten

Florent frowned. He would never have thought the lady had it in her to be nervous. That had obviously been a foolish supposition. Everyone had it in them to experience the full range of emotions, he supposed. But Lady Constance was not the type to allow those emotions to control her.

That wasn't to say she appeared controlled by anything but her will at the moment. Florent was quite convinced the woman had herself under a very tight grip. And that was the problem. She had appeared much more free and comfortable when he had first encountered her at the house party. Now she seemed almost brittle.

It was very strange. From the way her eyes kept flicking around and landing on that Wagner fellow, Florent couldn't decide if the woman was pleased or appalled at the man's presence. It made him suspicious of her and all the more determined to keep Daisy away from the beautiful, independent, young noblewoman.

Florent himself would prefer the man had never come, but he couldn't decide if it was a type of jealousy making him feel that way. The other man certainly garnered a great deal of attention from everyone, especially the female members of the group. Except his sister. Aside from her initial rather snide comments about the man, she barely seemed to take note of him.

That in itself caused him to worry a little more about Daisy, but he dismissed the thought. She had been clear in her view that Mr. Wagner made her instinctively distrustful, so that could explain her lack of interest in him. One thing you could say about his sister, Florent thought. She was certainly not wishy washy in her actions. If she didn't trust the man, she wouldn't give him another thought.

So, was he worried about Lady Constance having feelings for the strange new arrival? Florent hoped his disquieting thoughts were being kept to himself, but he couldn't be sure. He forced himself to interact with his fellow guests despite the feeling that he really didn't know how.

"How are things at Merton this year?" He knew estate affairs so felt confident he could have that conversation easily. And the viscount appeared personable enough.

"It has been a good year. The rains seem to have all arrived at the right times for our crops, so we are pleased. What about Alcott?"

"We could claim similar success, blessedly," Florent agreed. "You take your Seat, do you not? Do you find it hard to leave your estate behind for that long?"

Lord Merton raised an eyebrow. "No, why would I? Generations have been doing it. The lucky thing about the land is the crops will grow whether I watch them or not."

Florent laughed but heat climbed his neck. The man was right, but he had always felt the need to watch anyway, just in case. He was likely a fool.

"Of course, if you have many animals, I suppose you could have reason to need to give more attention. At

Merton we haven't been as focused on expanding our flocks as I've heard you've been doing."

The man's understanding put Florent a little more at ease.

"Have you found it to be worth the extra effort?"

Finally, Florent was on surer footing. This he was convinced of. "We have, so far, been very happy with the results. Our horses are starting to gain a reputation."

"Ah yes, I've heard of your hunters taking some recent prizes."

It took effort not to puff out his chest with pride. He nodded in acknowledgement, as controlled as possible.

"But still, with good enough stewards on staff, you should be fine to do your duty in the House when it's your turn," Lord Merton continued, in answer to Florent's original question.

"As I told your sister, though, a few days ago, I was late arriving in Town due to the state of the roads in my area. I hadn't realized that I hadn't left home in so long nor how the roads had deteriorated in the meantime. That made me realize, one has to remain aware of their surroundings, so remaining ensconced on your estate is a trifle short-sighted, in my opinion."

The heat returned to bother Florent's neck. That was nearly a direct hit upon him. He knew the conditions between his house and the village, that was the extent of it.

"So true," Florent murmured, wishing he hadn't approached that viscount first in his quest to find an appropriate husband for his sister. Or perhaps, he assured himself, anyone he started with first would be awkward. But he hadn't yet completely made a fool of himself, for that he would have to be grateful, he supposed.

"Mr. Alcott!"

Florent wasn't sure if he should be relieved or disappointed to be hailed thusly, but he turned with a polite smile to greet the one calling to him.

"Being formal, are we?" Florent greeted his neighbour and childhood friend, Viscount Adelaide.

"Apparently it is expected," the gentleman answered with a grin. "Wouldn't want to disappoint my lady."

"No, I suppose not, although your viscountess doesn't strike me as the most formal woman I've ever met."

Florent's childhood friend laughed and shook his head while he clapped his guest on the shoulder. "I'm glad you came, Flor, it's been much too long since we've spent any casual time together."

Florent grinned. "I know. It's hard to believe we're neighbours and all. We really ought to have been having regular dinners and such, at the very least."

"I cannot disagree with you, but there you have it, it's better that we're late than never."

"Better never late, I'd say," Florent grumbled, but it was in a half-hearted manner. He added a grin to make sure his friend knew he really wasn't offended. "It would seem marriage is agreeing with you."

"I do recommend it," Adelaide agreed with a grin and another clap to Florent's shoulder. "Perhaps my wife will find you one this week."

Florent had known in the recesses of his mind that was at the very least part of the purpose of this gathering, but he hadn't expected it to be stated quite that baldly, especially not by its host. It took effort not to frown. No wonder his brother hadn't wanted to come. While Florent was happy to enter Society at least a little bit, he had no intention of being leg-shackled on his first foray into such events. He still had plenty of arrangements to make before he really gave serious thought to marriage for himself. He was determined that this event be a success for his sister, no need for himself to be considered an option.

"Don't look so green about it, old chap," Adelaide told him, knowing full well what it felt like. "You're highly eligible now, you'll have to get used to it. If you don't get matched here, it will surely happen someday. Best you get used to being pursued."

"I suppose you had plenty of experience."

Adelaide grinned. "I did, to be sure. It had its moments of gaiety, but it was a dead bore much of the time. I can tell you, in that regard, marriage is certainly a relief."

"I could just continue staying home, I suppose."

Adelaide grinned again. "But where's the sport in that?"

Florent was growing tired of the interchange already, and he had only spoken with two people since he had set himself the goal of being more sociable. It was going to be a long week if he couldn't learn to enjoy himself. While he wanted to support his sister, and would remain if only for that reason, it was going to feel like one more chore on his list of things that needed to be done.

With what he hoped was a polite smile, Florent took his leave of his host and turned to survey the room once more. His mother and sister were mingling and appeared to be comfortable, much to his relief. If they were feeling as awkward as he did, there wasn't much he would be able to do to assist them since he appeared to be the most awkward person present.

The other new arrival, the one his sister thought looked like a rodent, Henry Wagner, was opposite him, seemingly deep in conversation with Lord Bathurst. That brought genuine amusement to Florent. The older gentleman was making sure to check on each gentleman present. From what Florent could tell from the man, though, he doubted he would be an acceptable candidate for Lord Bathurst's daughter. There was just something about the man that declared he was neither well-heeled nor a true gentleman. It struck him to wonder why the man had been invited. Ought he to have asked Adelaide? It might appear rude, but on the other hand, since he was Daisy's older brother, it was within his bounds to be concerned, wasn't it?

Florent resolved to keep an eye on things and ask later if he found another opportunity to speak privately with Adelaide. For now, he had no desire for an even more awkward conversation.

Flor had been informed that evening there was to be a supper followed by dancing. He again wondered if he should have stayed at Alcott. He hadn't danced in years. He hoped it was something you couldn't forget even if you were rusty. One more thing to make a fool of himself at. It didn't seem like he was going to be comfortable any time soon.

To his surprise, though, the supper passed quickly. He had been seated between Lady Isabelle and her mother. They had entertained him handily. Florent could understand a little why his mother was so delighted about resuming her friendship with her old companion. The woman was personable and charming. And her daughter seemed lovely if a little shy and quiet. Florent rather thought those might be endearing qualities in a future helpmeet. If only her father didn't seem so interfering. Florent wasn't certain he could bear up under such critical scrutiny for any length of time.

But then he glanced down the table to where he could see both his sister and Lady Constance holding their own courts. They were each vivacious and chatty without taking over their respective conversations completely. And he knew shy and quiet would be too quiet for him. There would be no conversation whatsoever if both the lord and lady were the quiet types.

He found it fascinating to watch his sister. Their mother had led him to believe that she was not succeeding in her Season, but it looked to him as though she thoroughly knew what she was doing. Or perhaps she was more comfortable in the country setting than she was in Town. He could fully understand that. Which led him to think that perhaps Lady Isabelle was the opposite to his sister. Perhaps she was more comfortable in Town.

"How have you been enjoying your time in London?" he asked her.

Her smile was sweet but fleeting. "Everyone is very kind, but it's a trifle too crowded for my taste," she answered him softly, not quite meeting his gaze. "Do you like it there?" she asked in a near whisper.

Florent had to quell an unexpected urge to laugh. The poor little thing probably was dreading being matched with any of the gentleman at the table if she didn't enjoy Town life. But she didn't really appear to be enjoying the country party overmuch either. So perhaps she was just a quiet person who preferred to be at home. He could fully understand that.

His eyes strayed toward Lady Constance once more. She would certainly not be content to remain in one place for the rest of her life, he was sure. He needed to stop thinking of her in such glowing terms.

Florent turned his attention back to the young woman at his side, realizing he still hadn't answered her question.

"I haven't spent a great deal of time in Town, to be honest, so I don't have a terribly strong opinion. I suppose I ought to get to know it a bit better as someday

I will be expected to take my place in the House like all those before me. But thus far, I have only made very brief visits to our great metropolis."

The girl nodded but kept her eyes on her plate.

She was much too young for this, he thought. Her parents should have kept her home another year. She wasn't ready for what they were expecting of her. His heart went out to her, but he had no desire to take on such a project, either. If he were to wed, it would be to take on a partner, not a parental-type role. The thought repulsed him despite having enjoyed both Bathurst ladies.

The laughter from the other end of the table drew his gaze once more and his eyes met those of Lady Constance briefly, and the breath stuttered in his chest. For a moment he thought she was actually beseeching him in some way, but for what he couldn't begin to fathom. On the surface she appeared to be having a grand time. He couldn't think of a single reason why he would have the impression she possibly needed his help. That woman struck him as being perfectly capable of anything.

Constance blinked, turned her attention back to her companions, and the moment was gone. But it lingered in Florent's mind, even as he went through all the motions of the rest of the meal. It was almost a relief when they all converged in the ballroom to the sound of the small orchestra tuning their instruments.

"Lady Adelaide has spared no expense, it would seem. She has arranged for a quartet from London to come and play for us this evening."

Florent grinned at his sister. "Are there no musicians in these parts?"

"None so elegant as these, I am told."

"Seems a trifle pretentious," he whispered into Daisy's ear making her snort, which had been his intention.

"Behave, Flor, we're all supposed to be impressed not judgmental."

"And are you?" he was curious, watching as she lifted a shoulder and pink tinged her cheeks.

"Perhaps I am tone deaf. It would explain why I was never the best musician myself. But I do not really hear a great deal of difference between these specialists and others."

"It's because you aren't too high in the instep despite being a nobleman's daughter."

Daisy seemed distracted and Florent was surprised to see her gaze following their hostess' brother-in-law who had only recently returned from Upper Canada.

"I thought you still hated Foster," he said, watching in fascination as she tried to hide a mixture of reactions from him.

"Hate is such a strong word, Flor. I suppose I've outgrown such a juvenile reaction."

Florent smiled even though his mind was working out all the ramifications of his sister's reaction. Had she developed feelings for their neighbour? That would be wonderful as he thought highly of the middleborn son of the household that was hosting them, except for the small fact that the man spent most of his time in the wilds of Upper Canada. He promised himself to keep a better eye on his sister and determine how she truly felt on the matter before he reacted.

And then he was distracted by the influx of their fellow guests into the ballroom. It wasn't quite a crush by London standards, but Lady Adelaide had invited gentry from the surrounding homes and there were enough people milling about to cause a hubbub and distract any mundane thoughts.

Not to say that Florent considered his thoughts mundane. Far from it of course. Unless he was thinking about his flocks. Even those he didn't think were dull, but he was well aware that others might not agree with his assessment.

When the dancing began, Florent partnered with Daisy first, as was proper, but he was soon partnered with every other available woman in turn. It was much more vigorous exercise than he ever would have thought, not having attended many balls in his life. The last time he had danced this much was when his sisters were learning. It was highly diverting but surprisingly challenging. Florent had thought himself very fit, so it made him question his own consideration.

"How do you manage to appear as though you've done nothing but sip lemonade all evening?" he questioned his next partner, who happened to be Lady Constance. His question brought on one of her tinkling laughs which he didn't object to in the least.

"Are you finding yourself winded by the exercise?" The laughter lurking in her eyes should have offended him, but he couldn't find it in himself to mind when she was so pretty and endearing.

"I am," he admitted sheepishly. "It's much harder than it looks. And all the ladies appear as though it is nothing for them."

"Do keep in mind that we are dressed much differently than the gentlemen. I would expect that would have something to do with it. We need to dance in order to keep from freezing in the current styles."

Florent chuckled over her words and had to force his gaze to remain focused upon hers rather than to linger on the expanse of skin she was referring to. A part of him wanted to tug on his cravat as she mentioned how very differently they were clad.

"Also, I would say most of the ladies present have a great deal of practice dancing whereas, I would surmise that you haven't danced in five years."

"That obvious, is it?"

Constance's happy burble of laughter sounded again but she shook her head. "Not in your steps but you mentioned you haven't been to Town since your oldest sister's debut. It seems in keeping with your dedication to your estate that you haven't been attending many assemblies if there even have been any in this area. It seems to me that everyone from the surroundings that Lady Adelaide invited is overly delighted to be here. So, I guessed there haven't been many such events."

Florent grinned. "Are you sure you aren't an agent for the Crown?"

"Why would you ask that?" she surprised him by the defensiveness in her tone. His eyebrows rose, even as suspicion followed them. *Was that where her association with Mr. Wagner came in?*

"You sound as though you would make a good investigator."

She lifted a shoulder in dismissal of his words. "Not really. I just look beyond the length of my own nose, which many people do not bother to do."

"That is a sad but true assessment. Except that they do look beyond their own noses when it is to sniff out gossip," Florent pointed out, making her smile return.

The steps of the dance separated them for a moment and strangely, Florent missed her. It was an odd sensation. He knew she'd return in just a moment. He had also really just met her, or rather was only just getting to know her. It was most odd for him to have such strong feelings about a near stranger.

Except she didn't feel like a stranger. He shook his head to try to rid himself of the uncomfortable sensations. But still, it was an effort to keep his smile within bounds when she returned to his side.

Chapter Eleven

Was her smile natural? Were her hands sweating?

And where was Mr. Wagner? She tried not to let her guard down, but it was hard when she found Mr. Alcott so very distracting.

Connie hoped her anxious thoughts were concealed behind her practiced social façade. Dancing with Florent Alcott was unlike any other partner. It was unsettling. Her heart fluttered most unnaturally. And she could barely stand being away from him.

It was ridiculous, is what it was.

She had never experienced such a breathless state while dancing. As she had told him, women of the ton were practiced dancers. It was not strenuous in the least. And they were not trussed up in cravats and coats like the gentlemen were. There was absolutely no reason to be short of breath. This particular country dance wasn't even vigorous, in her opinion.

And yet, she was breathless and tingly, and all sorts of unusual sensations flooded her. Perhaps the meat had been off.

But it didn't feel like a sickness. At least not an unpleasant one. The tingles and flutters she was experiencing, while new and unique, were pleasing and quite welcome.

Except that Florent Alcott lived on a country estate that he never, ever left. And he would be a viscount one day and probably be even less inclined to leave, except if he were to take his Seat in the House. How could she possibly be experiencing any sort of warm feelings for a man who seemed to be her exact opposite in every way possible?

It struck her as the oddest conundrum. But she couldn't argue with the feelings that flooded her as he directed their steps in such an adept way that when the notes of the song wound to a close, they were near enough the tall windows that they were able to slip out onto the terrace without causing any lifted eyebrows.

He danced her over to the edge without benefit of music, but she didn't pull away from his arms. It seemed she was attached to him, held by invisible threads that couldn't be broken, even if she had a mind to do so. Which she didn't.

Constance grinned up into her partner's face.

"You seem most skilled at that, Mr. Alcott. How many other ladies have you slipped onto the terrace with?"

Even in the moonlight she could see that he blushed over her teasing.

"Surely you must know I have no experience in such matters. You yourself were twitting me about my lack of practice at dancing."

"And yet you do it so well, despite that lack of practice."

Again, he appeared bashful over her words.

"It would seem the skilled partner makes all the difference."

"Do not sell yourself short, sir. From what I've seen of you, you are exceptionally good at whatever you do."

"How could you possibly know that?"

Constance grinned at the tone of his voice – a combination of doubt and hope that went straight to her heart.

"As you said, I have investigative skills," she explained with a laugh. "I've heard about your horses. And I experienced your dancing. I also overheard you explaining your cotton ventures. It seems to me you do not fail when you attempt something."

"That is quite the nicest thing anyone has ever said to me."

Connie flushed but still couldn't step away from him. She couldn't explain why she was so very drawn to the man. He was solid and safe. Things a younger Constance Moreland would never have considered attractive qualities but that she thought the most appealing now. Never mind that with his slightly tousled brown hair looking soft and thick and his earnest hazel eyes staring at her from a slender face that was just starting to show that he had left the care of his valet some time ago, he was one of the most handsome men she'd yet to clap eyes upon.

But she had met many handsome gentlemen in the time since she'd first entered Society. Connie was quite certain there was something particular about this specific man. It was unsettling and very unusual for her. It made her uncertain about where to put her hands and arms and what to say. She didn't know how to stand. Was she too close to him? Not close enough? Did she want to be closer or further? She didn't actually want the man to be courting her, did she?

Ever since her first unsuccessful Season in London, Constance had never actively wished to be courted by a man. Rather the opposite – she had often discouraged any gentleman who had seemed inclined to do so. And actively repulsing anyone who tried to force it upon her.

Yet here she found herself wishing for Florent to do something. What that something was remained a bit of a mystery to Constance, although she somewhat suspected it might involve a kiss. Despite her years and her many attempted suitors, Connie had never been kissed. She had used to compliment herself on that status as it was one sure way to ensure her reputation was intact and she wasn't forced into marriage.

But for the first time she rather suspected she hoped a gentleman would try to kiss her.

The flutters in her midsection and the continued dampness in her palms wouldn't have sounded pleasant if someone had tried to describe the sensations to her. It would instead quite sound like the onset of an unpleasant illness. But in that moment, experiencing the sensations, Connie thought it quite enjoyable despite the uncertainty that fluttered through her.

Constance Moreland had never been uncertain about anything in her adult life. But now she was. That wasn't the pleasant part. But the warm, fluttery sensation as Florent gazed at her in the moonlight, she would happily experience for hours or days even.

"Are you enjoying the evening?" he whispered.

"Immensely," she whispered back, not caring that she was probably grinning like a fool.

"Me too," Florent replied as his gaze ensnared hers and his head began to lower toward hers.

She had been right! Her suspicions that he might try to kiss her had been correct. She could barely breathe she was so constricted in her lungs from the wonder of it all.

"Ahoy there!"

Constance blinked and nearly groaned at the interruption. And her blood began to congeal to ice in all her limbs. That was Wagner's voice. Bile started to turn in her stomach, and she had to swallow hard not to vomit on Mr. Alcott's shoes. Perhaps all the fluttery feelings she had been experiencing before really had been the onset of illness, she thought rather weakly as she stepped away from Florent and turned toward the intruder.

Florent stepped in front of her in a show of protection. Constance was torn between finding that truly endearing and taking offence. She had never had a defender before. It was quite an unnecessary but novel experience. It brought a smile to her numb face.

"Mr. Alcott, is it? How do you do? We haven't yet had a chance to become acquainted. But I cannot allow you to be out here compromising my dear friend, Lady Constance."

She wasn't touching him, but Connie could feel Florent stiffen before her. She wasn't sure if it was at the suggestion that he would compromise a lady or the inference in Mr. Wagner's words about her being his dear friend. Either way, she felt her very new and nebulous dreams crumbling around her feet. With a sigh she stepped out from behind Florent's broad back.

"Mr. Wagner," she said in a less than pleasant tone. "I was surprised to see you here."

"So surprised that you could barely greet me, I noted," he replied in an aggrieved tone. It would have been amusing if it weren't so terribly disturbing.

"We are not friends," Constance explained in what she was trying to keep a patient tone. "And it was only days since we last spoke. I didn't find myself in any need to converse with you."

"That hardly sounds like the polite soul I have come to know, my dear lady." His tone made her feel the need to bathe it was so obsequious and set her teeth on edge.

"What are you doing here, Mr. Wagner?" She reworded her question to be more direct this time, hoping he might be more forthcoming.

"I was invited," was all he would say.

"Perhaps we should all return inside. As you said, it would not do to risk her ladyship's reputation."

Florent sounded so formal that Constance felt like weeping, which was an unusual reaction for her, but everything about the sojourn at Everleigh was unusual so she oughtn't be surprised. Still, she felt despondent as she accompanied the two gentlemen back into the ballroom. She couldn't even find within herself to care if others took note. As Florent seemed to imply, being in the company of both gentlemen was sufficient to protect her reputation from much damage.

"Thank you for the dance," Florent murmured politely but distantly as he took his leave of her. At least he did her the favour of keeping himself between her and Wagner so she could make good her escape.

Or perhaps it hadn't been intentional, she couldn't be sure. In either case, she was highly uncomfortable, but she was determined that no one else would know from looking at her.

Peggy, of course, could tell.

"I'm so sorry, my lady. I saw Wagner interrupted your little *tete a tete* and I was too far away to do anything about it."

Connie appreciated that Peggy was doing her best to keep her word to stay by Connie's side. But since she had been dancing just before the interruption, she couldn't possibly be expected to have done anything to help. She hoped her smile wasn't as sad as it felt.

"Thank you, my dear Miss Smith. There was little you could have done." She swallowed her disappointment and tried to brighten her smile. "I have been distracted so haven't been paying attention. Have you been enjoying your evening?" Connie then lowered her voice and leaned closer. "Has your swain been entertaining you?"

Peggy blushed. Connie had never seen her do such a thing before. It made her look lovely and young and in that moment, jealousy swept through her. But Connie quickly dismissed the unwelcome and terribly unkind sensation. She was happy for her friend. She refused to be jealous. Connie had made her choices and would stand by them whether others changed their own minds or not.

"He's not my swain," Peggy insisted in a low voice that did nothing to hide her delight over the prospect, making Connie laugh.

"Very well, whatever you're telling yourself, have you been kept occupied this evening, my dear?"

"Occupied yes, but some of it has been preoccupation with your whereabouts, I'm afraid."

"Oh dear, I suppose we should have discussed that in the ballroom I was most likely safe. Although, as it turns out, that wasn't entirely true."

Peggy bit her lip and looked around the room. "Perhaps we ought to leave after all," she said, disappointment sounding as though it were nearly choking her.

"I will not allow the likes of that weasel to make me run away. What good would that do me, after all? I'll then be running for the rest of my days. Hardly a comfortable way of life, to my way of thinking."

"But what else can you do?"

"Just keep myself out of his clutches long enough for my questions to be answered. Surely someone will be able to tell me what is going on and how I can avoid his machinations."

Despite the dire nature of their conversation, Peggy laughed lightly over Connie's words even as her gaze shifted past her and pink hued her face once more.

Connie resisted the urge to turn and verify that Lord Merton had come into view. Her stomach clenched. How lovely it must be to be Peggy in that moment. Nausea filled her as she fought the sensation of jealousy once more. She was being a selfish beast to begrudge her friend and family member such a pleasant future. Not that she was begrudging it to her, it was just an inconvenience. And she wasn't even upset, she assured herself. It was merely awkward timing. But if not for Mr. Wagner's arrival, it wouldn't even be all the awkward. It was perfect timing for Peggy to find love, as a matter of fact. They were near enough to Connie's home that she could do without a companion for the brief time necessary to arrange her affairs.

But Henry Wagner had followed her, and that changed everything.

While Constance had no intention of ruining Peggy's chances, Connie had to protect herself for the time being, at least until she could verify what exactly was going on with Mr. Wagner's presence at the house party. It was entirely possible she was being unforgivably self-centered to think his presence had anything to do with her. She doubted it, but it was possible.

"I'm truly sorry, Peggy," she said, just loud enough for her companion to hear.

"There is nothing at all for you to be apologizing for, my friend. If nothing else, we are family, however distant. I could never leave you to fend for this situation on your own. Have no fear. It will all come out in the wash eventually."

Connie couldn't help smiling over the quaint expression. She wasn't certain she could be confident that anything to do with Wagner would come out in the wash as Peggy promised, but it was a somewhat comforting thought nonetheless.

"Perhaps you ought to approach Lord Merton," Peggy whispered.

"Lord Merton? Why? He's your suitor."

Peggy smiled. "Not necessarily. And if he is so unsteady that he cannot keep his head when another woman speaks to him, then he is not for me, anyway. Even if that woman is as beautiful as you. Surely there will be other beautiful women on earth."

Constance grinned. "Are you using me to test him?"

Peggy giggled. "We might as well use this situation to accomplish something useful."

Connie wanted to hug her companion in that moment, but she still didn't have any desire to draw any more attention to herself than necessary, so she restrained the impulse. "You are a dear and I so appreciate you." She thought for a moment. "Perhaps we could together approach the gentleman and then neither of us are left unattended nor left out of the conversation."

"That sounds perfect."

Constance immediately suited her words to actions and skirted the dancing couples to join Lord Merton, who was momentarily standing alone. She trusted that Peggy was by her side as she was afraid to look around to make sure as she didn't wish to make eye contact with anyone, especially neither Mr. Alcott, nor Mr. Wagner.

Arriving by Lord Merton's side, Connie dipped into a polite curtsy.

"My lord, how do you do this evening?"

His eyebrows rose slightly but he didn't comment on her rather bold approach. It was a house party after all, they couldn't possibly be expected to stand on ceremony in such an environment.

"I do well, thank you for asking, and yourselves? Lady Constance? Miss Smith?"

Peggy bobbed another curtsy in response to his question but held her tongue, expecting Connie to take over the conversation. Connie's heart constricted a little. She ought to be the one sinking into the background in favour of her companion but under the circumstances, she just couldn't do it. A small smile lifted the corners of her mouth. Really, were there any circumstances in which she would slip into the background, she wondered. Perhaps it was a skill she should make an effort to cultivate.

Chapter Twelve

Florent watched with what felt like a jaundiced eye as Lady Constance and her companion approached Lord Merton. Was she to start flirting with the viscount too? Florent had understood the woman had chosen to forego marriage in order to travel the continent. And he had never received the impression that she was of loose morals. And yet, here she was flitting from man to man throughout the party, barely spending any time with other ladies. It gave him pause in thinking that she was so unique and special that he might endeavor to change her mind about marriage. He didn't know what to think about anything anymore and certainly not the curious Lady Constance.

The one time Florent had entered Society and taken an interest in a woman, and it backfired badly. Bile churned in his belly before he called himself to task. He was being much too hard on the poor woman. Was that not the purpose of the Season? For men and women to pair up and make matches? Florent suspected that was the very reason why neither of his brothers had been willing to accept Lady Adelaide's invitation for that week. They refused to be matchmade. Florent had thought he felt similarly but then had been so drawn to Lady Constance. Now, though, the thought of her curdled in his mind. He was so instinctively repelled by the newcomer, this Wagner fellow, that he was far less interested in Lady Constance if she were a particular friend of the man.

Of course, Lady Constance's reaction to the interruption on the terrace had been less than enthusiastic, Florent reminded himself, striving for a balanced view of the matter. He ought to make an effort to remain as neutral as possible until all factors became clear. He prided himself on being fair and balanced in his judgment. Now was not the time to change that tendency, no matter the provocation.

Still, though, watching her pay attention to another gentleman did not sit right with him, so Florent determined to turn his own attention elsewhere. There were many appealing young women present that evening. Lady Adelaide had invited several of the neighbouring families to join the house party for the ball that night. It would be churlish of Florent not to dance with all the daughters present. These were his neighbours after all.

He had to suppress a grin over his own perverse thoughts as he bowed over the hand of the first young lady he came to. Perhaps he was just as flighty as Lady Constance.

"Miss Alwin, it's a pleasure to see you and your family here this evening."

His grin dimmed slightly when the girl simpered. He had known her all her life, and now she was simpering at him. This was why he dreaded Society, he thought as he tried to keep his smile in place. As he had said to himself, he had known her all her life. She wasn't usually the simpering sort, as far as he could tell. It was possible she was nervous. This was probably one of her first Society events, and it was possible she wouldn't get many more opportunities. And he couldn't walk away now that he had just greeted her. He finished what he had started.

"I am almost certain the next dance is to be a minuet. Might I have the pleasure of you as my partner?"

Thankfully she had reduced the strength of her glee and merely nodded politely, he was relieved to observe. Perhaps it wouldn't be so bad after all to partner with her.

The music filled the room and he swept her into the dance. No longer simpering, the young woman merely appeared delighted.

"Is this your first time at Everleigh?" he asked her after they had settled into the steps.

"It is," she answered shyly.

"My sister's, too," he told her.

"Really? I would have thought with you being direct neighbours, that she would have been here regularly."

"I was, of course, as a lad, playing with all the boys. But since there were no ladies living here at the time, none of my sisters ever set foot in Everleigh until now."

Much to Florent's amusement, the young woman almost preened under this knowledge. But then she seemed to call herself to task and brought the unattractive reaction under bounds.

"Is it ridiculous that this information adds to the excitement of the occasion?" she asked him with wide eyes.

"Not ridiculous, I don't suppose. It makes your invitation all the more special knowing how rare it is, doesn't it?"

The girl's vigorous nodding almost dislodged her curls, and Florent almost found it endearing. But then his gaze encountered Lady Constance in the expert arms of Lord Merton, and it was all he could do not to trip over his own feet.

"How has your family been, Miss Alwin? Is everything well at home?"

"As well as usual," she replied simply. "There has been an uproar in the house about tonight, of course. And some in the family will always find something to complain about, so not very much has changed."

"Will you be going to Town for any of the Season, do you suppose?"

"It isn't likely unless the cotton pays off better than was even expected," she answered simply, and Florent's heart went out to her. She was gentry and would thus be accepted into Society if she could get herself there, but without a sponsor, or a windfall as she had mentioned, her family wasn't likely to be able to afford the expense. "Regina is prettier than me, so Mama says she'll get the Season if there's only one of us can go."

Flor had to work hard not to allow his jaw to unhinge over her matter-of-fact statement. To her it seemed acceptable, but he couldn't see how she could accept such an odd way of viewing things. Although, was it really so odd? He supposed the family had to weigh the costs and if they truly thought they could only go once, they would have to make the choice that made the most sense for their family. He just hated the thought that it was being decided on something so arbitrary as beauty. He couldn't remember what that sister looked like, so obviously she had never struck him as a paragon of beauty. Not that he'd ever been paying particular attention, but he did have eyes in his head. Surely if she was a diamond of the first waters he would have noticed.

"What will you do?"

"I might become a teacher or a companion, maybe even a governess."

Florent blinked. "Would you enjoy any of those occupations?"

"Probably," she answered him with a smile. "In either case, enjoying it or not, I need to do something, don't I? As the oldest of so many children, I need to make way for the others. And I cannot be an expense any longer than necessary."

Florent could completely understand the sentiment as he had always experienced the same ones. But surely it was different for him as the brother and heir. Surely a gently bred young woman should be looked after by her family all her days.

He wasn't prepared to offer for her himself, but he could only hope that dancing with her might have drawn the other gentlemen's attention to her. And it turned out to be a correct guess. The young woman spent the rest of the evening dancing with a different partner each time. He didn't pay too close attention so he couldn't be certain if anyone's attention was more marked than the other, but there was a slight possibility the girl would find her match after all.

The rest of the evening passed in a blur. Florent almost allowed the entire ball to complete without dancing again with Lady Constance, but he realized that might be too pointed. Yes, she had offended him, but that was his problem, not hers. Her behaviour wasn't so out of the ordinary. It was his reaction that was the unusual element. He shouldn't make it obvious to his friends and neighbours. And really, he didn't want her to know she had bothered him either.

"Lady Constance, might I have the pleasure of the next dance?" he asked, making her an elegant leg. He was probably doing it rather too brown. He didn't have to be dramatic about it, especially not after their most recent encounter.

One of Constance's agile eyebrows rose to a peak, nearly disappearing into her elegant hairstyle but she didn't say anything, merely putting her hand into the one he was holding out to her.

"You have been avoiding me," she commented pleasantly as they swept into the steps of the country dance. Florent nearly faltered in the pattern as her words registered.

"I beg your pardon." He meant it as a question as though to ask her to clarify, but she smiled coolly, as though she were considering not granting her pardon.

"You heard me plainly, I am sure, Mr. Alcott, you are just trying to wriggle out of answering for your actions."

"And which actions might those be?" He thought to tease her, even though he shouldn't. He thought her questionable due to her friendship with Mr. Wagner, but he really had no foundation for such suspicions. He didn't believe in intuition. Florent's lips twitched with grudging amusement. The lady had a point that he couldn't dismiss, he had been avoiding her. But he would make a valiant effort anyway. He couldn't very well tell her his true thoughts. Without waiting for her to come up with something else to say, he added his excuses.

"There are many neighbours and acquaintances present with whom I have not socialized much. I owe them my attention this evening since they will most likely not be present the rest of the week."

"Hmm." Her response was noncommittal, as though she accepted his words but didn't believe them. But her eyes also looked sad despite the sweet but subdued smile upon her face. Again, Florent had to suppress an inappropriate urge to comfort or protect her. The woman was an intelligent companion and he enjoyed conversation with her. But he had no desire to be part of a pack of gentlemen vying for her attentions.

He managed to guide their conversation into neutral territory and the dance passed pleasantly enough. Her gaze was watchful as he bowed over her hand in farewell when it came to a close. Florent had no desire for her to search his thoughts with her piercing gaze. He kept his smile as generic as possible as he took his leave of the beautiful woman and went in search of his sister.

"I haven't seen much of you this evening, Daisy dear. Are you enjoying yourself?"

"Immensely. What about you? From what I've observed, you have made every heart in the county pick up its pace."

Florent laughed over his sister's exaggeration. "Better to be prolific than specific, I would say." But then he blinked over his words. Was Constance doing the same as he had done? Perhaps she wasn't being vulgar, she was merely spreading herself around so that no gentleman would get the wrong idea. Except that he had. He had thought there was something special or unique in their interaction. It was disconcerting. And terribly judgmental on his part to fault her for the very thing he had done as a means of protecting himself. It was entirely possible she was doing the same.

And when he reflected upon her lack of reaction to Mr. Wagner's greeting again, Florent had to admit she had not appeared overly eager for that man's presence. Florent had judged her harshly because he had an aversion to the newcomer. That was unfair on his part. But still, she was evidently acquainted with the oily gentleman, besides the fact that she obviously didn't fit in with his provincial life. She was not for him, he reiterated to himself.

Really, Florent assured himself, he needn't be thinking anyone was for him at this point. It was time for him to experience a little bit more that Society had to offer before he made such a permanent choice for his life. Just as he had told his sister, he didn't want her rushing into any decisions, he oughtn't to do so either. When Daisy returned to London, he would accompany her for at least a week or two and really see how she fared and what all was involved in the Season business. That ought to give him a better idea of what he could consider for his own future.

But he couldn't really muster a great deal of enthusiasm for the prospect. And it was all Lady Constance's fault. Why did he have to go and find the least appropriate female the most appealing?

Florent turned his back on the very unhelpful thought. He was going to give her the least amount of thought possible. He would be as polite as he could manage during the house party and then he would never see her again.

With effort he brought his attention back to his sister. "My apologies, Daisy, I was wool-gathering."

"They seemed to be rather heavy thoughts for such a light-hearted occasion."

"Is it truly light-hearted, though?"

To his surprise, Daisy's grin only brightened. "It truly is, Flor. You ought to try it. You will become truly ensconced in your old stick ways if you aren't careful."

Florent laughed as he knew Daisy was expecting, but he feared she might be correct. This made him even more suspicious that she was up to something, and he tried to assure himself that he would keep a closer eye on her even as he tried to enjoy the house party.

Thus resolved, he finished out the ball, polite to everyone, smiling where appropriate, and then gratefully tucked himself into bed with a sigh of relief. Two days down. He could surely survive a few more.

The next day dawned sunny and bright. A perfect day for country pursuits. The assembled guests were all pleasant company, and Florent really had no reason to find the shine had gone out of his existence.

When he entered the breakfast room, thinking he would have it quite to himself, he was surprised to find Foster and Daisy sitting side-by-side with their heads close together as though sharing secrets like schoolchildren.

"Good morning," he called curtly, irritated at feeling as though he were interrupting a private interlude. "Ought you to be this private with my sister, Frost?"

His question only caused Daisy to giggle before Foster touched her elbow and got up from the table. Florent was just about to take his sister to task for her forward behavior with their neighbour when they were joined by other guests seeking to break their fast.

The morning was filled with conversation and laughter as the guests milled about the public rooms of the grand house and spilled out into the gardens. Just as nuncheon was announced, Florent was surprised to see Foster ride into the Everleigh courtyard with his father, Lord Alcott, beside him grinning.

"Father, I'm surprised to see you here. I thought you couldn't get away from the House of Lords."

"This forward young man wrote and requested that I post down as quickly as possible, so here I am."

Florent, ever aware of her presence, heard Connie's gasp even though she was across the lawn from them. Her wide-eyed expression nearly distracted him from the matter at hand, but it also confirmed the premonition he had been suffering under all morning.

He was somewhat relieved to note that his sister wasn't nearly as hoydenish or forward as he had begun to worry, but Florent wondered how he could have been so distracted by the other guests that he hadn't noticed his sister was falling in love with the man she had claimed to loath since they were children.

Lady Adelaide took matters over and assembled everyone in a withdrawing room for the announcement as footmen poured wine with bubbles for everyone to join in the joy.

"I have the privilege of announcing that Lord Alcott has agreed to grant me his dearest daughter as wife," Foster pronounced to the gathered nobles. No one appeared surprised since Daisy was clinging to his arm like a besotted limpet.

Foster tried to stifle his disgruntled grin as he wondered if limpets really could be besotted. He was being decidedly churlish. He ought to be as delighted as everyone else seemed to be. He was, he insisted to himself. He most certainly wanted to see his sister happy, and she appeared to be deliriously so. Once the initial hubbub died down sufficiently, Florent made every effort to get into the spirit of things as he embraced Daisy to congratulate her.

"You pulled the wool over everyone's eyes," he remarked, watching a grin split his sister's face.

"Even yours?" she asked with wide eyes, striving for innocence.

"I knew you must be up to something, but I couldn't have fathomed this. I should have, though. I even remarked upon it the other evening to you, noting that you didn't seem quite as indifferent to the gentleman as you've tried to profess through the years."

If possible, Daisy's grin widened, and she looked so happy Florent almost had trouble looking at her, like she was the sun and he would be blinded looking directly at it.

Florent watched his sister's face turn pink and she leaned in closer to him. "I'll tell you a secret."

His eyebrows inched closer to his hairline, but he leaned even closer to hear what she had to say.

"I thought I hated him," she admitted. "But it turns out, I've always loved him. And he's going to take me on the best adventures. He even let me in on other secrets. Things I ought to tell you about but not now."

Florent stared at his sister and wanted to insist she tell him what she was hinting at, but then she was pulled away from his side. A flurry of activity followed the announcement because along with their engagement was also the news that Foster intended to take Daisy with him when he returned to his holdings in Upper Canada, even if temporarily. The pair were so in love they couldn't bear to be separated even a few months. So, a special license was to be procured and the wedding held at Everleigh as the culmination of the house party.

Florent watched in amusement as Lady Adelaide preened over her success. Not only had a match been made at her party, but it would actually end in a wedding. For the lady's first social event as hostess, no one could argue her success.

For the briefest moment, as Florent scanned the room and all the gathered well-wishers, his gaze collided with Lady Constance's. Hers was bright and watchful, and she appeared to be pleased for the newly engaged couple just as everyone else. But when their gazes meshed, she blushed prettily and turned away as though he had caught her in a thought that he couldn't decipher. He also couldn't decipher the pleased feeling that filled him for the briefest moment.

Of course, he told himself as he turned back to the matter at hand, it was pleasure for his sister, not anything else. And Florent was happy for his sister. He truly was. Although it sounded even to his own mind that he might be protesting too much. It shouldn't need stating. Of course, he was happy for Daisy. And Foster, too, he might add. They had been chums as children and even managed to stay in touch through a very occasional letter through the years.

But Florent suspected there might be a slight tinge of jealousy in the jumble of feelings that he was trying to swallow down. Of course, he was happy for the two, but he also felt more alone than ever. Daisy was his favourite sister. He would miss her. Alcott would feel even more empty with only him and their parents rattling around within it.

He knew Daisy was an excellent correspondent, but it would never be the same once she wed.

"Do promise you're happy for me, Flor," Daisy implored when they had another moment of quiet together, as though she could read his troubled thoughts.

"I swear it to you, little sister. But now you swear you truly are as happy as you seem, and he hasn't tricked you into anything."

Daisy laughed right in his face. "Is there any question I'm nearly bursting with happiness? This is exactly the perfect situation for me. We are hoping to put down roots here abouts, too," she assured him. "Frost has already spoken to an agent about finding us somewhere to live, perhaps in the village or the surrounding countryside. We will have to travel, of course, to see to his interests in various parts, but we'll have a home here."

"And you're up for these travels, Daisy? I never knew you to have wanderlust." Aside from his slight case of envy for the adventure ahead of her, Florent was actually concerned for his sister's well-being. But she only sighed happily and grinned.

"I never would have actually thought I was the most adventurous sort, Flor, but it turns out that I am. I cannot wait to set sail, as a matter of fact. I do want to return and have a settled life eventually, or at least a certain semblance of being settled. But knowing Frost, we'll always have certain ventures on the horizon."

"And you are certain you are fine with that?"

"More than fine, as a matter of fact." With that, Daisy put her hand into his elbow and started to lead him further down the path they were walking on while he questioned her. "While we're talking about adventures, though, I do need to tell you something."

Florent stiffened slightly, causing her to laugh lightly.

"Don't get stuffy, Flor, or I won't tell you." She paused for a moment before correcting herself. "Actually, that is an empty threat as I feel duty bound to tell you, since I'm certain it affects Alcott and probably others in the area."

Now Florent was confused and concerned. "What is it?"

Daisy bit her lip, obviously hesitant, so Florent put his free hand over hers where it rested in his elbow. "I promise I shan't ring a peal over you, but you have to tell me if it affects Alcott."

"Of course, I'm just girding my loins as it were. It's how I came upon this information that will make you unhappy. Well, that and the information itself, of course. You see, there has been smugglers in the area. And they're smuggling cotton."

"Oh sweet, merciful heavens! Are you sure? Tell me what you know."

"Don't get too upset, Flor. The good news is that Gilbert Northcott is supposed to be arriving today or tomorrow, I wasn't too clear on that detail, and he'll have customs agents with him. They are intent on shutting it down. But there's currently no way of knowing if they've been active for long or what sort of damage they might have done in the meantime. And I think there's really no way of knowing if the customs agents will actually be able to shut it all down." She nearly stumbled over her words now in her haste to get the entire tale told. "Since you've started trying cotton in some of your fields, and I'm certain others have, too, I feel like it's more important for us to make sure it's completely taken care of. But I'm afraid Gilbert might just be concerned about Everleigh lands."

Florent frowned, pleased with his sister's wisdom and sharing her concern. But then he thought of other details. "Gilbert Northcott is a good man, and I have reason to suspect his interests in the matter might go deeper than just protecting his own family's lands. For one thing, how does he know where to find himself customs officers?"

He was pleased to see that Daisy was paying heed to his words as she puzzled over what he had said. "I suppose I can see your point. Although, I cannot begin to fathom why he would have knowledge of such things. Even Frost didn't know where to start to find the local magistrate when we first discovered the smugglers."

Frost's gaze narrowed on his sister's face. "That brings us to the other matter of concern that you referenced – how do you know about these matters?"

He watched with a grin as colour flooded her face. "Keep in mind I'm not your responsibility anymore, Florent," Daisy said pertly.

"You are until the settlements are signed, so you'd better get talking."

She must have been able to tell there was little heat in his words as she laughed again.

"Very well, Flor, but you did promise not to ring a peal, don't forget." She paused for a moment to gather her thoughts. "I saw them. The smugglers. Arriving with a shipment in the middle of the night in the cove out behind the moors."

"In the middle of the night? What in heavens were you doing on the moors in the middle of the night? Have you lost your mind? I'm going to wring Foster's neck for him."

"No, you aren't, Florent Alcott. You promised not to get angry."

"I promised not to get angry with you, Daisy, not your swain. How can I entrust you to him if he cannot prove to be trustworthy?"

To his shock, Daisy laughed. "I love you my dearest brother. And I love that you want to protect me. But use your head a little more and you'll realize it wasn't Frost's fault. I followed him. He certainly didn't invite me."

Florent's jaw dropped open. "Keep talking. I want to hear the entire story."

As Daisy's tale unfolded, Florent found it harder and harder to grasp what she was saying. There were smugglers in Kent County. And somehow his young sister was having a hand in apprehending them. Of course, she wasn't so young anymore if she was getting married that week. And it wasn't so very strange for Kent to have smugglers, he supposed. But he would never have expected them in their part of the county, despite their being so close to the mouth of the river. It was just too far to be convenient for the criminal element. But he supposed it also made it inconvenient for those tasked with the assignment of apprehending said criminals.

"So, you have to keep it a secret for now," Daisy concluded her explanation.

"A secret? How am I supposed to do that while I question our staff and tenants?"

Daisy laughed. "That's how, you don't do that. You stay here at the party for a few more days, until I wed, in fact. And then you can carry on with whatever you'd like to do. But for now, you'll have to leave it in the agents' hands."

"You know leaving my concerns for someone else to care for is not very much in keeping with my traits."

"I do realize that, Flor, but just this time, you're going to have to. If you go about questioning people without really knowing what is involved, you could end up warning the criminals we are hoping to apprehend."

"I do hope you are using the word *we* metaphorically. I do not want you anywhere near this."

Daisy's smile tightened with his words, but Florent couldn't retract them. This was his sister. He could not bear for anything to happen to her. It would be hard enough allowing her to set sail across the Atlantic with her husband. Until they were wed, she was still very much Florent's responsibility, and he would not allow her to mix herself up with criminals.

"I do not see how you think to stop me, for one thing, Florent, my dearest brother. For another, I shan't actually be doing anything. I was very much using *we* as a collective term. Meaning all of us, really. Gilbert will be arriving with the agents, and they will do whatever agents do. While I don't know much, I do know that just as you do not want me involved, you cannot involve yourself either. We need to leave it to them. For now, at least."

Grudgingly, Florent could see the wisdom of her words. The day passed surprisingly easily despite the worries that had piled onto his mind. Lady Adelaide carried on with her planned entertainments, and most of the guests were none the wiser about the investigation underway around them. They rode into the village for some shopping and took luncheon at the local inn, thus bringing needed business to the area. Florent had to admire their hostess' wisdom. It also allowed time for the agents to arrive and get themselves set up in the servants' quarters and the loft of one of the barns. One who appeared to be higher ranking than his fellows, joined the guests for supper that night. To balance out her numbers, Lady Adelaide invited Miss Alwin back to join her guests.

The murmur in the receiving room rose to a crescendo when it was revealed why Officer Cordon was present. Florent watched everyone as attentively as possible. Of course, most of the guests were from other parts of the country and were merely curious about the increased numbers, but Miss Alwin was from these parts in addition to him, his sister, and their mother. She also appeared as surprised and curious as everyone else, but what surprised Florent the most was Henry Wagner's reaction.

The man gasped dramatically. Flor would have thought it was fake if not for the immediate absence of any other reaction. If he hadn't been watching for people's response, if he hadn't been warned by his sister, he might not have even noticed Mr. Wagner's odd behavior. Florent tried to keep his balance; he recognized that he was already looking for reasons to distrust the man, but this felt like genuine reason to be distrustful.

Flor's sharpened gaze also took in Lady Constance's lack of reaction to the entire thing. Her face merely displayed a very minor interest, as though the entire situation was a mere spectacle laid out to amuse the assembled guests. That would have been amusing if it were not so very distressful.

Chapter Thirteen

Nausea flooded Connie's entire being and she had to swallow hard not to allow the bile that threatened to make itself shown. Every other ounce of her effort went toward keeping a serene smile upon her face. Henry Wagner was probably involved in this smuggling that everyone was so up in arms about. That would explain why he was there. She hadn't yet been able to get a straight answer out of him as to how he had finagled an invitation, nor had she found the courage to ask Lady Adelaide.

But now she didn't have to. She instinctively knew it was the case. There was nothing she could do about it though, aside from make even more certain she didn't somehow find herself forced into marrying him. That would just put the final nail in the coffin of this dreadful day.

The look on Florent Alcott's face as their gazes had collided would forever be etched into her memory. He had come to the exact same conclusion as she had about Mr. Wagner. The only problem was, as the disdain in his face had indicated, he thought she was somehow involved.

Connie stifled a sigh. Apparently being a spinster also meant she was guilty of every other vile thing people could imagine.

It wasn't fair. But then, life rarely was. Just the fact of her circumstances told her that. Why had she received the inheritance from her grandmother while her distant cousin Peggy was left to fend for herself?

Well, perhaps Peggy wasn't to be left to fend for herself for much longer if the attention Lord Merton kept paying her was any indication.

Clearly Constance Moreland was a more romantic soul than she ever would have imagined if even in the face of her current tragedy she could be seeing roses and bluebells in such an arrangement. Connie was happy for her companion. She truly was, she insisted within the confines of her own mind. It would be perfectly wonderful for Peggy, and it might even be more interesting for Connie to have a new companion. Peggy had been becoming increasingly despondent in their travels. A new companion couldn't be worse than that.

But, despite herself, Connie would miss Peggy. And she was just the tiniest bit envious despite how happy she was for her friend. The vision of Lord Merton bending his head to hear something Peggy was saying was also etched in her memory for all time. It had been lovely and meaningful even if Peggy was merely remarking upon the weather or the drapes or whatever she had said. Just knowing the tall, handsome nobleman had exerted himself to pay attention to Peggy was lovely to behold.

Everyone should have someone willing to bend for them, Connie thought rather poetically even as she fought a sense of devastation. Obviously Florent Alcott was not the bending sort. Or at least he had no intention of bending for her – a woman he thought capable of being in league with smugglers.

Not that there was yet any evidence to support the supposition that Wagner might be involved. But if Florent didn't tell the authorities about the possibility, Constance would have to do so. It was only right. She was likely the cause of his having been invited, even though she couldn't fathom how he had gotten himself tied up with a smuggling gang. But Connie wouldn't put it past him. She had never had reason to suspect him of actual criminal behaviour before, but it had always been clear to Connie the man was not to be trusted.

Of course, no woman would trust a man trying to ruin her into marriage.

That in itself should be considered criminal. Sadly, in their Society it was not. It was just an alternative way of accomplishing your goals. But Connie would never allow herself to be put in that position. And now she was in a different awkward position. Thankfully, she doubted Florent would actually give voice to his suppositions about her. He was one of those gentlemen who would consider it dishonorable to besmirch a woman's good name.

Florent Alcott was a rarity.

But that didn't stop him from having his own suspicions about her. It was silly that it hurt her feelings. There was no reason for it to do so. They had made no promises to one another. Not even the promise of friendship. But she had thought they were friends, and now her feelings were devastated.

She was being a fool. And Constance Moreland never acted like a fool.

Connie lifted her chin and kept her expression serene. No one would know from looking at her that the bottom had dropped out of her life.

"Are you well?"

Connie nearly jumped out of her skin. She hadn't noticed Peggy's approach.

"Of course, I'm well, why do you ask?" Connie would rather jump off the battlements in that moment than admit how she was feeling.

But Peggy wasn't fooled. She stared at Connie with an elevated eyebrow. When Connie only returned her stare, Peggy's questioning expression dissolved into one of concern.

"Allow me to rephrase, then. I know something is wrong. Tell me how I can help. Is it Wagner?"

Connie's heart swelled at the fierce expression on her friend's face. Despite the fact that she was certain the young woman would be leaving her employ in the not-too-distant future, Connie knew Peggy cared about her and would stand by her side as long as needed.

"All is well, but I would appreciate your company, thank you."

"Can you believe the various developments of the afternoon? A betrothal and soon to be a wedding? How deliciously romantic. What a thrill to be here to witness it unfold."

Connie managed not to roll her eyes. "There's also the small matter of smugglers infesting the neighbourhood."

Peggy frowned. "But that shan't affect us, surely."

"Not even with the government agents right under our noses and underfoot as well, no doubt."

Peggy's frown intensified. "Why does this bother you? I would have thought you'd find it even more fascinating than I do."

Constance shook her head. "Forgive me, my dear. I am out of sorts is all."

"No, you aren't," Peggy argued. "You are never out of sorts." Her gaze was searching as she stared at Connie once more. "This troubles you for some reason. I know you couldn't possibly be involved, so I'm not sure why it would. Have you some of your funds invested in cotton or something? Is that why this bothers you?"

Connie laughed, surprising them both. "I hadn't actually given that side of things a single thought, but I think you might actually be right. I have even more reason to be disturbed than I thought."

"Then tell me what it was before I brought that up. How can I assist you if I don't know?"

Connie sighed but she leaned her head closer to Peggy's ear to ensure there was no way she would be overheard. "I don't have any evidence of any wrongdoing, but I have a terrible suspicion this is why Wagner is here."

Peggy was suitably silenced before the implications came home to her. "And you fear you'll be tainted by your faint association with the bounder. But no one has connected you here, have they? I mean, aside from your suspicion that it is because of you that he was even invited, that is."

"He acted proprietarily toward me last night after I shared a dance with Mr. Alcott."

"Oh dear. I am sorry, Constance."

Connie lifted a shoulder in a brief shrug. "What can you do? If the man is so staid and straight that he cannot consider another side to his own suspicions, I have no interest in him anyway."

"That is brave of you to say, but I'm sure it still hurts your feelings if anyone would have a suspicion about you."

"Nothing has been said so perhaps I am reading overmuch into a single glance."

"Your hunches are nearly always correct, I'm sad to say in this instance."

"I know," Connie agreed with a soft sigh. "But on a much happier note, I cannot think there is anything to be suspicious about your Lord Merton. He seems quite delightful."

Peggy took the bait of changing the subject and a grin bloomed on her face. "He is, isn't he? No, I cannot think there is a single suspicious thing about him."

"Aside from what he is seeing in you, though, right?"

Connie had meant it as a teasing jest, but her poor companion took it straight to her heart. "I know exactly what you mean, I have been wondering the same myself these past two days."

"Do not be a ninnyhammer. You are the loveliest creature, and he would be lucky to have you to wife. I was merely funning and well you ought to know it."

Peggy's grin belied the reaction she had made Connie think she was having. "And I was funning you in return. That should teach you a lesson not to mock others in their time of high emotions."

Connie laughed immediately. "Lesson duly noted. And I thank you for the moments of levity. They were exactly what I needed." They shared a fond glance. "Which is exactly why you did it," she concluded with another affectionate smile.

"Now, tell me, what do you suppose the household is going to do about all these goings on?"

"I have no idea about that, but I do know that we're going to have to do something."

"We? What could we possibly do?" Peggy was aghast at the very thought, and Connie saw her gaze flicker toward Lord Merton, which caused a strange twist in her gut. Already Peggy's loyalties were drifting elsewhere, which was, of course, as it should be, but it still left Connie feeling sadly isolated.

"If you'd like to involve him, you are free to do so," she offered in a low voice, watching as Peggy blushed and glanced in his direction again.

"To whom do you refer?" Peggy asked with a sly smile and a light giggle. "Besides, until we decide what exactly we're doing, involving him might just scare him off. As I'm sure you're aware, nothing official has been said or asked or declared."

Connie's smile felt sad. It was all so melancholy. Even Peggy's life was left up in the air at this point. She needed to be rid of Henry Wagner, then she needed to see Peggy settled, and then she would go home to her parents for a little rest while she figured out the direction of the rest of her life. Perhaps her life of wandering was a little too unsettled even for her at this stage of life. She couldn't prevent her eyes from flickering toward Florent Alcott where he stood congratulating his sister. She wasn't certain she wanted to be that very settled, but steadiness would be nice right about now.

Suddenly she felt as though her existence were tremulous and insecure. It had always felt like an adventure before, but now she had begun to wonder why she had ever wanted to wander the globe in the first place. Perhaps she just needed a nap.

Connie sat a little straighter in her seat and pulled back her shoulders even more than they already had been with her usual proper stature.

"We are going to help with the investigation. Or at least offer our hostess some help with the visiting agents. That might afford us a little bit of access to the information, don't you suppose?"

Peggy appeared skeptical even as she nodded. "I can see that it might. But do you think we ought to involve ourselves? It sounds like it might be dangerous."

"With the agents here, it ought to be nearly as safe as a walk in the park. Besides, I don't think we need to involve ourselves to the point of danger. Just to the point of gleaning information," she concluded with a grin.

Peggy's eyes flickered once more toward the tall gentleman who was still standing beside the fireplace.

"Go ahead and consult with your suitor, my dear," Connie offered kindly. "I likely won't even need your company if I approach our hostess first, so this needn't besmirch you in any way."

Peggy scowled. "I'm not concerned about being besmirched, my lady. You are my primary concern. Of course, I will remain by your side."

Connie grinned despite the seriousness of the situation. It was good to have ones you could depend on, even if you had to pay them. That thought almost tripped up her enthusiasm, but she refused to allow herself to be distracted. This was her life, and she would make the most of it that she could.

The guests began to disperse to prepare for supper, and Connie took the opportunity to approach Lady Adelaide. She knew the woman would probably be preoccupied with preparations, but it was the best time to not be disturbed by other guests.

"My lady, might I have a word?"

"Of course, Lady Constance, how can I be of assistance?" Despite what was likely a harried situation, Connie was impressed with their hostess' presence of mind.

"I would like to help with the investigation." Connie didn't bother dancing around the topic.

Lady Adelaide stared at her for a moment before a grin spread across her face. "How delightful," she said, causing Connie's eyebrows to rise. Was the woman daft?

While Connie was determined to be involved, she had expected some sort of resistance to her offer.

"I am not completely certain how the gentlemen will feel about our involvement, but we shall insist," Lady Adelaide said, putting her hand through Connie's bent elbow. "Politely, of course, in such a way that they shan't even realize. Let us strategize after supper," she continued, with a grin.

Connie's heart lifted somewhat. It seemed to her as though she didn't have much to look forward to, so suddenly she was much more optimistic about her future. At least an adventure of some sort, and of a different variety than her travels. Excitement started to fill her. But she wasn't certain what else to say to her hostess.

Lady Adelaide squeezed her arm where her hand rested in the crook of Connie's elbow. "We shall discuss it later. Right now, I have things to do in preparation for the supper and no doubt you do as well. But I promise, I shan't forget."

Connie was most pleased with the other woman and happily allowed her to disengage and slip down a hallway. Turning back to Peggy, Connie was able to settle in beside her with complete equanimity.

"You look rather self-satisfied," Peggy observed with wry amusement.

"I suppose that's appropriate since that's how I feel, but I probably ought to hide it a little better," Connie replied with a grin.

"Quite," Peggy replied with a roll of her eyes as they climbed the stairs to their adjacent rooms. "What has you suddenly looking so pleased?"

"I shall tell you once we're private," Connie whispered, and Peggy appeared suitably chastened.

"I do apologize," Peggy said as soon as they were in Connie's room with the door closed.

"Don't be a goose. I just didn't want to announce it on the stairs. You know how sound can sometimes travel in these large houses."

"Which is why I apologized."

"But there was no harm done so no need," Connie insisted before hurrying to explain herself. "I spoke with Lady Adelaide while you were distracted with making calf's eyes at your suitor."

"Do say you're jesting. I would never be so bold nor so vulgar."

Connie laughed. "I might argue that statement but it's not the point. Her ladyship said that she and I shall insist on being included in the investigation. I'm nearly beside myself with delight."

Peggy stared at her friend. "I cannot fathom why. You are a strange, unnatural creature, my dear lady."

Undeterred, Connie laughed again. "You are entitled to that opinion, and I shall even forgive you for it."

"But, Constance, what if you run into danger? And what if Mr. Wagner really is involved, as you suspect? And what if he draws you further into scandal?"

"Wouldn't it be better to find out if the bounder is involved? I already have no intention of allowing the man to court me, but all the less if he is involved in criminal activities," she explained patiently. "But what do you mean by asking about drawing me in to FURTHER scandal? What scandal has he already drawn me into? I thought we had done quite well at keeping my name from any reproach."

"Well of course we have, but not for lack of the man trying. By involving yourself into this question, you are only risking yourself. Quite needlessly, I might add."

Connie knit her lips together and began to pace about the room. She didn't want to argue with her companion, but she also couldn't accept her assessment of the situation.

"I can see that you might have reason for concern. But I don't think this is a needless endeavour. I do not have any desire to be a quiet, biddable female. I plan to live my life on my own terms, just as I always have. I do not see how you think this is any different."

"I suppose you are right, it isn't really any different than when you took it into your head to start travelling the world and declaring yourself a spinster at the ripe old age of twenty-one summers. As it stands now, you're still not to the age that many ladies don't yet consider themselves on the shelf. And yet you've been travelling for years now." Peggy shook her head despite the fond smile on her face. "You are most unnatural, my dear."

"I know. But keep in mind I have no intention of being like either of my sisters."

"No, but surely there has to be a happy medium. For one thing, you would have the wisdom to choose more wisely than either of them did."

Connie sighed. "You think I ought to wed. But, Peggy, I ask you, who should I choose? Not that there is a queue of eligible men applying for the position." She offered a self-deprecating laugh before elaborating. "From what you know of me, what sort of gentleman do you truly think would be able to make me content if I were tied to him for life?"

"I think a sturdy, steady gentleman who could offer you a different sort of adventure," Peggy stated immediately before her smile twisted into a rueful one. "I cannot elaborate on that as I cannot say what sort of adventure that would be. If you were to wed, there would likely be children that followed, so I don't think you could carry on traipsing about the world as you have been, so it would have to be some other sort of venture." She began pacing along with Connie, tapping her chin as she thought. "Perhaps one of these agents. Not that I would wish to see you pursuing a life of danger, but I could see you being quite good at investigations. Or perhaps a scholar, if he were studying something that you might enjoy."

Now it was Connie's turn to tap her chin. "You make some interesting suggestions. I will have to give it further thought. But I think you must have been talking with my family to come up with ideas of how to convince me to remain on English soil."

Peggy laughed but shook her head. "Not a bit. I'm just wishing to have my cake and eat it, too. If I do manage to find myself in a situation with a home and family of my own, I selfishly would like to have you nearby and not have to worry about you traipsing about the world without me."

Connie allowed her mouth to drop open dramatically. "Peggy Smith, are you trying to say you will miss our travels?"

"Perhaps a little," she answered grudgingly, making Connie laugh delicately.

"Well, those are troubles for another day. For today, I would love to find out that Henry Wagner was a criminal and that he would no longer be nearby to bother me."

"Would you really?"

"Don't you think that would solve some of my problems?"

"It might cause others," Peggy pointed out, but Connie refused to accept that.

"I cannot allow people to paint me with the same brush as him. Just because he is determined to marry my inheritance doesn't mean I actually wish to have anything to do with him."

Peggy laughed lightly. "Very well, I concede defeat for now. How can I help?"

"You needn't involve yourself in the least, but if you could try to hover near me or at least keep your eye out for me so that you can defend my reputation if he were to make an unwelcome move, I would deeply appreciate that. For now, I do believe I ought to be reasonably safe here at Everleigh. I cannot imagine Lady Adelaide would take kindly to anyone being compromised on her watch."

"Perhaps not, but there has been a sudden and surprising betrothal no one seems to have seen coming."

"But there is no scandal attached to that."

"That is exactly the point, though, isn't it? Mr. Wagner would be delighted to become betrothed to you in order to avoid scandal."

Worry nibbled at Connie's stomach. It was the age-old problem. The man wouldn't leave off his pursuit of her or rather the pursuit of her pocketbook. It was exactly why it would be nearly perfect if he were to be declared a criminal and carted off to Botany Bay.

"Never mind," Peggy said suddenly. "I swear I shan't allow it to happen. I will glue myself to your side if need be."

Connie laughed. "Nothing so dramatic will be necessary. Instead, I shall glue myself to Lady Adelaide's side." They shared a smile before Connie turned to the practicalities. "Ring for our maid, we must dress."

Chapter Fourteen

Florent knew himself for a fool. He had no reason to harbour any sort of suspicions toward Lady Constance. Just because Mr. Wagner claimed previous knowledge of her did not mean either of them were involved in this smuggling scheme that Foster and Gilbert were bringing to the attention of the landowners in the area.

Smugglers in the county was certainly a worry, though, just as his sister had pointed out. They were trying to cultivate cotton at Alcott. Smugglers bringing in the same product in order to avoid the import taxes could greatly impact his profits and those of the others who had decided to try the exotic crop like he had. Some of his neighbours had imitated him and started small, to see if they could make a success of it. He had taken the greatest risk as this was his second year of trying it and had decided to plant extra fields with the finicky crop. So far it was thriving, and he had reason to be confident.

The English thirst for velvet was going to keep him in the cotton business if he could keep the fragile plants alive. But not if smugglers undermined him with bounty from another land where it grew more easily and cheaper. Even if they caught these criminals, there would be more following in their wake. It was always the way of the underworld.

This wasn't like bringing in French brandy. Many in England were now trying to grow cotton, whereas no one was really able to successfully replicate the French liquor. Besides, the brandy was the sort of thing many had brought in for their own use. From what Daisy told him of what she had witnessed on the beach, it sounded to Florent as though there were many bales of cotton, perhaps enough to impact his own trade since it was unlikely what his sister had found was the first or only shipment. He was never that lucky.

He couldn't wait to discuss the matter more thoroughly with the earl, as well as his own father. They would be sure to have a level-headed view of the matter.

It didn't really matter if Lady Constance was involved with any plots or not, Florent assured himself. Such an exotic flower was not for him anyway, so it was merely a matter of interest, not a matter of the heart. With a slight smile and a shake of his head, Florent realized his thoughts had become missish. Perhaps he had already spent too much time with debutants, and he had only been at Everleigh a couple of days.

The day after the big revelation as to what Foster and Gilbert, two of Lord Adelaide's brothers, were investigating, most of the guests went off to explore some old Roman ruins on one of Everleigh's properties while Florent, Gilbert, and Adelaide accompanied the Customs Agents to the caves where Foster and Daisy had seen the smuggled cotton bundles.

"I still can't believe your brother allowed my sister to involve herself in this," Florent complained to Gilbert as they rode.

"You don't know much about your sister if you're saying something like that," Gilbert countered with a chuckle.

Florent laughed, too. “I suppose he couldn’t have stopped her. But one of you ought to have warned me what was going on.”

“There wasn’t time or opportunity. By the time you were around, Foster had already handed the matter back to me, and it was no longer truly a concern for your sister, nor something you needed to worry about.”

“And yet here we all are traipsing about the moors heading to explore some caves,” Florent pointed out. “Clearly it is something that affects me, my family, and my lands.”

Gilbert laughed again. “My apologies, old chap, I was referring to your sister, not the cotton. Daisy is Foster’s to worry about now.”

Florent’s stomach seemed to drop out from the bottom of him. He didn’t much care for even an old friend claiming ownership of his sister.

“Better don’t let her hear that,” Florent warned but Gilbert only chuckled again.

“It seems to me both your sister and my brother are quite happy with their new ownerships. Just as Daisy now belongs to Frost, he belongs to her. That is the way it ought to be, and you should be happy for it.”

Inexplicably, Florent wanted to plant his old friend a facer and he couldn’t decide if it was caused by an urge to protect his sister or if it was jealousy motivated. In either case, he moved away from Gilbert and hurried to catch up to Adelaide and the Customs Agent who seemed to be in charge of the whole matter.

“I cannot guarantee that we’ll catch anyone or everyone, my lord,” Florent heard the agent saying. “With all of us traipsing around, it is sure to have become known to the criminals.”

“But my brothers have identified some of the locals involved. Surely you can question them.” Adelaide would brook no argument nor any failure to clear out his lands, it would seem. Florent wanted to applaud such an attitude.

"Of course, we will, I just cannot guarantee the success rate."

"You are not filling me with confidence in our Majesty's ability to hire capable men for the tasks assigned," Adelaide commented drily, making the agent cringe.

"Leave off, Adelaide," Gilbert called out to his brother. "Everyone will do the best they can, and we'll get the matter sorted one way or the other. It may not be immediate. But it will be taken care of, you have my word."

Florent's sharp gaze fastened on his childhood friend. "You seem more invested in this than I would have expected."

Gilbert just grinned and didn't explain himself further.

Florent caught back up to his noble neighbour, Adelaide. "If I understand their strategy correctly, they plan to try to catch the criminals in the act of clearing out their bounty from here. But if that doesn't work or if they don't catch everyone, which is the most likely scenario to my mind, then they will leave some of their agents in the area to continue the investigation. It is likely that they will move off from Everleigh lands and probably leave Alcott alone too after they're caught here. But whatever is left over of the gang will regroup and move somewhere nearby, most likely. Criminals aren't usually terribly hard working nor remarkably intelligent, from what little I know of the underbelly of mankind. They will stick with what they know and understand which, unfortunately in this case, means they know these parts, so that tells us some of our neighbours are involved."

Florent understood Adelaide's reasoning and his heart sank at the thought of his neighbours being criminals. Or even perhaps some of his tenants. That would be the worst. It would feel like a personal betrayal.

"You're being quieter than usual," Lord Adelaide commented from atop the horse at his side.

"I'm just pondering what we think we're going to accomplish when we get to this cove the agents have been guarding. I have to admit to you, Adelaide, I think we might have been foolish for coming on this errand. Your brother and his associates seem to have the matter well in hand. We should have accompanied the others."

"Are you really that eager to explore a bunch of mouldering old stones, Florent?" Adelaide demanded, laughter lurking in his tone.

"Not in the least. But if your suspicions are correct and that Wagner fellow is involved in this, we shouldn't have allowed him to accompany the others."

"How could we have stopped him without revealing our hand?" Adelaide demanded.

Florent shrugged. "Well, maybe we couldn't have stopped him, but at least one of us should have gone with the others."

"Foster will look after your sister," Adelaide assured him.

"I'm sure he will, but Daisy isn't the only person in your wife's company. And if I'm not mistaken, your wife is in an interesting condition. Why on earth did you allow her to go off with someone you have suspicions about?"

To Florent's shock, Lord Adelaide laughed. "For one thing, I have a tendency to have suspicions about everyone, so my wife would never stand for me trying to stop her from doing what she wants to do merely based on my suspicions. For another, there are enough footmen and outriders accompanying her ladyship and the guests that I'm actually somewhat surprised Wagner even went with them. Surely, he's not such a dunce that he didn't notice."

"I didn't," Florent pointed out sheepishly, "so it's possible he was distracted as well."

"Criminals notice this type of thing, Florent. The fact that you didn't reveals your innocence, not your lack of intelligence. But now I must ask, what has you so distracted? Surely, it's not still concern over the estate. From what I've seen and heard, you've turned Alcott around completely."

"To the dismissal of everything else there might possibly be in life," Florent added dismally, causing his friend to laugh and stare.

"You sound terribly glum."

"Don't mind me," Florent waved away the viscount's searching gaze. "We have other things to consider right now. If I'm not mistaken, we are nearly to our destination."

Adelaide cast him a knowing glance that Florent did his best to ignore.

As they climbed down the trail that led from the moors to the beach, Florent pushed as many thoughts from his mind as possible. He couldn't allow thoughts of Lady Constance to linger in his mind at this time. But he wondered if asking about Henry Wagner might be helpful.

"Adelaide," Florent called out.

"Yes?" the viscount asked with a slight grin.

"How did Mr. Wagner come to be invited to your wife's party?"

To Florent's surprise, Adelaide muttered an unacceptable word and shot a glare over his shoulder toward his brother. "You'd have to ask the spare."

Despite the gravity of the current excursion, Florent laughed over his friend's teasing of his younger brother. Since Lord Adelaide was heir to the Earl of Everleigh, his brother Gilbert was the spare. It had occasionally been a source of contention between the brothers when they were boys, but Florent had thought they had accepted their roles in recent years. It would seem it was still a way for Adelaide to express his discontent toward his brother without going into detail. Gilbert, though, had grown steady in his reactions since they were boys and didn't do anything other than smile over his brother's words.

"Is there something I ought to know, Gilbert?" Florent persisted.

"In the course of our investigation into the possibility of smuggling being hidden on Everleigh lands, his name came up. So, I thought it might be helpful to have him at hand when we brought things to a head."

"At my wife's party," Adelaide exclaimed. "Without warning either of us that there was the possibility the bounder was dangerous."

"He's too lily-livered to be dangerous," Gilbert countered in what was probably supposed to be a soothing tone. "There is nothing to worry about from that worm. He's greedy, not dangerous."

"But what of the ladies?"

"Some could be in danger from him but not likely of the physical sort of danger."

"That is not comforting," Lord Adelaide expostulated. "My wife has invited ladies here in the hopes of matching them up suitably. Having a fortune hunter present does not set anyone at ease."

"I promise we'll have it all wrapped up soon," Gilbert soothed.

“Not soon enough to suit my wife,” Adelaide growled, and it was all Florent could do not to laugh despite the gravity of the situation. Again, he thought of Lady Constance.

“What of the ladies who came from the continent?” he asked just as they arrived on the beach and set off to explore the caves.

“Lady Constance and her companion?” Gilbert and Adelaide said almost simultaneously. “What of her? Are you having an eye in those quarters?”

Florent ignored the question, only answering part of it. “She seems to be an associate or at least an acquaintance of Mr. Wagner. Is there reason to suspect she might be involved in the scheme?”

“Not as far as I can tell. From what I know of the lady, she is intelligent but too soft hearted for her own good. Wagner has been pursuing her, and she hasn’t yet managed to dissuade him.” Gilbert paused and shook his head. “This is the reason why ladies aren’t supposed to start traipsing about the world without a male escort. It has nothing to do with their capabilities. Well perhaps a little, but not their worthiness or intelligence. They just aren’t able to properly defend themselves. If she isn’t careful, one of these days she will be caught by one of these cads who is just after her money. And then she’ll be stuck.”

Florent opened his mouth to ask further but thought better of it. Despite Gilbert’s assurance that she wasn’t involved and that she was only being pursued by the bounder for her money, Florent wasn’t prepared to make any sort of declaration. Perhaps he had grown old and staid. Changing his ways was going to take some effort.

“What are we looking for?” he asked instead.

“Your sister and my idiot brother left the cotton here. Which wasn’t the idiotic part. That was as it should be.

We didn't want to alert the criminals any sooner than we had to. But now I and the Customs officers want to see it for ourselves."

"So, we're here to verify that the cotton is still here?" Florent persisted, wondering why they were all needed for this activity.

Gilbert shrugged, nodded, and grinned at Florent's seemingly incredulous reaction.

"Did you think we'd be catching them in broad daylight, then? What did you think we were coming here to do? Would you have rathered to go off and explore the ruins with everyone else?"

Heat climbed up the back of Florent's neck. As a matter of fact, he probably would have preferred that. This didn't seem like it was going to be a terribly productive use of his time. He would rather be watching over Wagner. That prompted his next question.

"Who is keeping an eye on Mr. Wagner? If he's truly under suspicion, should we be leaving him to traipse about with our women?"

"You don't have a woman to worry about, Flor," Gilbert pointed out with a chuckle.

"Have you forgotten that my mother and sister are with your wives?"

"Foster is more capable than you'd expect," Lord Adelaide answered soothingly. "Your sister will do well with him."

Florent tried to agree with the viscount, but it was hard to think of the boy he'd known growing up as a suitable mate for his favorite sister. For any of his sisters really. It was hard to see any of the Northcott boys as grown-up men when he'd known them since they were all snivelling boys playing with frogs. He couldn't help but laugh at the direction his thoughts were going in.

"It's hard to accept that," Florent excused.

"I know. Believe me," Lord Adelaide said. "I've been struggling to accept that any of us have turned into men, including you and me."

They shared a grin just before they entered the first cave.

"It's just as Frost and Daisy described," Gilbert called out, making Florent clench his jaw over the reminder that his sister had involved herself in something so dangerous. "Don't be angry, Flor," Gilbert added. "She did a good thing."

"You don't have sisters; you can't possibly understand."

"That's true," Gilbert agreed with a grin. "But I needed help with this, and she gave it without my even asking."

"Would you have asked a gently bred woman?" Florent was aghast.

"No," Gilbert responded immediately. "But after the fact, rather than being upset about it, I can see my way clear to be happy that she did. Being angry is only going to complicate matters. I did ask my brother to look into things while I wrapped up something else. I don't necessarily agree with his methods, but he got it done." Gilbert paused for a moment and then cast Florent a knowing glance. "I might add that we all know your sister and her inability to stay out of things."

Florent couldn't argue with that, so he kept his mouth shut and his lantern elevated as he approached the covered mound in the back of the cave.

He had almost not believed it could be real. He had never known a true threat to his livelihood in all the time he'd been working to right his family's financial situation. It felt for a moment as though he had been kicked in the stomach – something that had once happened to him when he had been training a horse.

That hadn't been the horse's fault and had therefore not felt so personal. This felt very personal. Someone was threatening him and his family. It didn't matter that the caves weren't on Alcott land nor that he didn't yet know if anyone at Alcott was involved. Everleigh hadn't yet started to experiment with cotton, so it wasn't nearly as personal for the Earl.

Florent wasn't sure if he felt like weeping or raging. He would never cry, so rage would have to be uppermost. Not that it would help. He took a deep breath to quell all reactions. Becoming any sort of emotional wasn't going to help them clear this matter up.

"What can I do?" he asked quietly.

Gilbert didn't pretend to misunderstand his question. "Agents have already gone to Alcott to ask around."

Florent was shocked. "Why didn't you ask me?"

"Because you were coming with us. And it's better if you aren't there. It's much more likely the agents will get more candid reactions than if the lord is present."

"But I'm not the lord," Florent protested.

"Not yet, maybe, but you're as good as in this case. I promise we'll keep you appraised of whatever is said or takes place, but it's better this way for the first steps. Then, based on what the agents find out, you can take the next steps on your own lands. The same is being done with all the landowners hereabouts. This isn't personal, Florent."

"It feels very personal."

Gilbert's smile was almost condescending, and it put Florent's teeth on edge. But they had known each other since they were children, so Flor tried very hard not to plant the man a facer.

"I know this can't be enjoyable for you, and I'm sorry that it's happening. But would you rather we had never found out?"

"No, of course not."

"So, it's just uncomfortable right now. That will pass. And you'll be relieved when it is over."

"I would rather it had never happened," Florent burst out and immediately regretted the impulse as heat crept up his neck. He didn't sound the least bit reasonable. After a deep breath, his face transformed to a rueful smile as Gilbert just stared at him, not really reacting in any way to his outburst.

"Of course, I do realize that's a futile wish. And I'm trying to appreciate your involvement. I suppose I would be entirely ineffective on my own if I ever would have even found out about this criminal venture in these parts. Which I might not have if you and your brother hadn't gotten involved and my sister hadn't stuck her nose into it." Florent scratched his head and headed toward the entrance of the cave, leaving the agents to their investigation. He wouldn't really have anything to add despite his seeming intelligence. "How did you get involved, by the way? You haven't been home in weeks, as far as I know."

Gilbert was keeping step just behind him, and Florent heard his low chuckle.

"For such an intelligent man, you don't take note of certain details, do you Florent?"

Flor wanted to bristle over the statement but since he had just been thinking nearly the same thing, there wasn't much he could counter it with. So, he shrugged.

"I know everything about my land and animals and tenants. Although now I'm starting to question if I know my tenants as well as I've thought. So, you are probably correct on all counts. I ought to say I *thought* I knew everything about all there was to know in the region." He shook his head as he stepped into the sunshine. "So, what are you saying I haven't been paying attention to?"

Gilbert laughed. "I'm not a customs officer, but these gentlemen are my colleagues."

Florent frowned. "That doesn't make much sense. You either are or you aren't. Don't make me feel even more daft than I evidently am."

Gilbert laughed again. "I do various things for the Home Office."

Florent stared at the man that he thought he knew well. A man he'd known since childhood, since they played on these very beaches with their tutors and younger siblings in tow. And he felt like he was looking at a stranger.

"Is this a new development? Why didn't you ever tell me?"

Gilbert shrugged. "I'm telling you now."

"But probably only because Daisy involved us."

Gilbert laughed lightly. "Perhaps. Florent, you've been tied up with straightening up your own family's affairs. As your father's heir, I couldn't really ask you to be involved."

"Why not? Is it that dangerous?"

"It can be."

"So, Adelaide didn't know?"

Gilbert side-stepped that question. "I told as few people as possible. I'm sorry that you feel betrayed now. But it wasn't a personal affront. I couldn't tell anyone. Until something like this happened, and even then, I am most often able to deal with matters without divulging my personal involvement. But this time, because we've been friends for so long, I'm trusting you with this detail."

Florent frowned at his friend but then nodded and clapped him on the shoulder. "Well, I cannot say that I like anything about this situation, but I suppose I'm glad that you're involved. It's not likely Adelaide or I would have even noticed. And it could be a problem for many of us in the area. So, thank you." He chuckled. "And I apologize if that sounded grudging. It wasn't meant to be."

With his childhood friend's chuckle propelling him out of the cave, Florent allowed his mind to wander back to the ugly conversation he'd had with Constance before they'd parted earlier that day. It had been brief, but it still unsettled him that he could be so suspicious of a gently bred young woman.

"How do you come to be acquainted with Lady Adelaide?" he had asked her that morning at the breakfast table while he was finishing his coffee and she had just begun her meal.

Her fork had stopped halfway to her mouth and for the briefest moment the elegant and graceful young woman appeared awkward, as though unsure whether or not to put her fork down or continue with taking the bite she had intended. Her gaze flickered around the table as if to determine if anyone was paying attention to their conversation or perhaps even if someone were going to rescue her from the uncomfortable situation he had thrust upon her. Guilt assailed him but he felt righteous in his indignation toward her.

After a brief blink that seemed to wipe away her awkwardness with her long eyelashes, Lady Constance finished putting the food in her mouth and lowered her fork. Taking a moment to wipe her lips delicately with the napkin she had in her lap, after chewing briefly, the lady swallowed and sat back in her chair, never relaxing her very proper posture. Her gaze remained challengingly enmeshed with his but the expression on her face returned to one of pleasant conversation.

"We met during my debut, Mr. Alcott, thank you for asking. She has been kind enough to remain in touch with me by letter even during my travels. I cannot express to you how delightful I have found her missives to be wherever they find me."

A sliver of doubt threatened to crack his determination, but Florent was undeterred.

"Really," he drawled, half in question, half acknowledging her words without having to alter his question.

"Yes, I would swear I could almost smell the scent of the countryside from her descriptions at times. Her ladyship is an excellent correspondent."

"Did you feel unsafe travelling here from the continent? Is that why Mr. Wagner accompanied you?"

Again, there was the briefest hesitation while her gaze widened, and she shot him a glare before she resumed a pleasant mien.

"What would make you think he accompanied me? Just because we might have travelled from the same general direction does not mean we did it together," she pointed out with dignity. "I have never felt unsafe while travelling. Except perhaps on a particularly stormy sea or some such," she added with a light laugh. "I was actually surprised to encounter him here, as I was expecting a small, exclusive selection of guests."

Florent, despite his being impressed with her deft handling of his question, forced a light laugh. "It would seem Lady Adelaide's taste in associates is quite eclectic."

He had allowed the inference that she was included in that assessment, much to his current shame. As he thought of the conversation, it was all Florent could do not to squirm visibly.

He was a donkey's hind end. There was no other way to put it. Well, there were other ways to put it, but Florent tried not to be excessively vulgar even in his own thoughts.

He had allowed his usually clear judgment to be clouded by an intelligent woman's beauty. And he couldn't even explain to himself why that was. It wasn't as though he had a bad experience in his past to explain his reaction. He had so little experience at all, either good or bad. And that was why Florent almost smacked himself in the head as realization struck.

The next hour seemed to drag, but it was just as he had suspected. The noblemen were most definitely surplus to needs on the operation. Gilbert Northcott and his customs agent associates had the matter well in hand and as soon as he was able, Florent headed back to Everleigh House. He wanted to at least be present when the others returned.

As the afternoon waned on, he felt increasingly concerned about Lady Constance. Of course, he was concerned for his sister and mother, as well, but he couldn't shake his conviction that Connie might be in danger.

He couldn't believe he had suspected her of involvement with the cad, Henry Wagner.

And cad, Florent was certain the man was even if they hadn't yet found hard proof other than the testimony of two of the smugglers they had apprehended before Florent had left the men to their work.

While they were in the back of the cave well past the bales of cotton that were already found, looking to see what else could be found before they had to leave if the tide turned, four agents approached with two scruffy men struggling between them.

"We found these two out back trying to turn tail when they saw us."

Gilbert immediately took over and Florent could see that the man hadn't been jesting, he truly was a professional agent. He never would have suspected his childhood friend of such capabilities.

"Tell us what you know, and we'll make sure your punishment is deportation not decapitation." Gilbert had said it in so matter of fact a tone that the two hadn't fully understood at first but when the other agents explained in far rougher terms what fate awaited them, they became far more forthcoming than their original belligerent attitude had implied.

"It was him," they both said almost simultaneously, pointing their fingers at each other. Florent would have laughed if the matter weren't so deadly serious.

Gilbert patiently drew the information out of them.

"How was it him? Do you mean he invited you into this involvement?"

The scruffy pair exchanged glances and didn't at first answer. Neither Florent nor Gilbert recognized the men personally, although Flor thought they had an air of familiarity about them.

"Let's start with this, how do you know each other?" Gilbert continued. Florent just wanted to knock their heads together and drag the information out of them, but he held silent.

"Know'd him since we was boys, guv'nor," one finally said while the other nodded vigorously. "Prob'ly before we was even born."

Gilbert didn't comment on the improbability of that but continued his questioning.

"Are you from around here?"

"My gramma lives in these parts, and I visited her every few months my whole life. We," he gestured between him and his friend, "grew up in Martinon. You might not know it guv'nor, it's out of the way from anything interesting, a few villages away from the main roads."

Gilbert chuckled as the man surely had intended proving him to be the professional Florent was not. He was still fighting the urge to knock their heads together and could only stand back and watch. Finally, with a bit more roundabout questions, Gilbert started to get to the information that mattered.

"And so you were finding life in Martinon too boring for your tastes? Is that correct?" The men nodded vigorously again, nearly hypnotized by Gilbert's soothing tone. "How did you get involved with cotton?"

"Never knowed it was cotton, guv'nor. Such a mamby pamby thing to smuggle, don't you think? We thought it was going to be of the liquid variety, don't you know? But that fine, fancy gentleman's gentleman told us how much we'd be greasing the wheels with and we was in, don't you know?"

"Which gentleman's valet, exactly, if you wouldn't mind sharing?"

Florent almost snorted. Gilbert was so polite. Flor was nearly certain it was Wagner's. From what he had seen, he was the only one whose valet looked even better dressed than the nobles. It was all he could do not to march off the beach that instant. Wagner was surely involved, and he was with Florent's women. He ignored the fact that in his mind, Connie was included in that classification.

That was enough for Florent to know he should have been more concerned about the ladies that morning. He never should have agreed to accompany Adelaide. Even though, as a future landowner in the county, he was, of course, concerned about any criminal activity, he couldn't bring himself to be more worried about that than the actual people in his life.

Not that Connie was really in his life. Especially not after the cold way he had treated her that morning. He would be lucky if she would even speak to him, let alone offer her forgiveness.

Florent had been so convinced that he was above everyone else. But he was nearly as caddish as Wagner himself.

When the carriages that had taken the guests to explore the ruins didn't return within an hour of Florent's return to the house, he strode back out to the stables and asked for his horse to be saddled. Careful questioning of the grooms and ostlers assured him he knew the route the excursion would have taken. He rode out to find them.

Chapter Fifteen

Lady Constance simmered. There was no other word for it. Despite Lady Adelaide's promise that they would be able to join in the investigation, here she was with the rest of the guests riding to explore some ridiculous ruins.

Who cared about a bunch of rocks that had once used to be a house or fortress or abbey or some such thing? The here and now was of much more significance and interest to Connie than something that might have happened hundreds of years ago.

She didn't much care if she was being ridiculous. She was angry and annoyed and if pressed she might admit that she was even a little afraid. It had been evident to her that Florent Alcott suspected her of being involved in whatever plot they were all investigating. She herself knew that she was innocent of any charges that could possibly be leveled against her. But Florent had struck her as such a steady, level-headed, even kind, man that thinking he suspected her of criminality was unsettling and made her question whether or not she would be able to defend her innocence if she didn't get herself involved.

Lady Adelaide had promised and yet here they were.

Connie didn't know how to ask her hostess about the change of plans without turning shrill or emotional and causing a scene in front of the others, so she had kept her own council for the time being.

And so, she stewed and simmered. And worked up a great head of anger.

How dare Florent Alcott judge her? Who appointed him a judge of her? What right did he have to think she might be a party to anything nefarious? And upon what grounds could he possibly base such a suspicion?

Connie wanted to weep and rail but instead she put up her parasol to ward of the sun and smiled as benignly as she could upon the world around her. She managed to gather her roiling emotions into her bosom and keep them there, turning her attention to the other occupants of the carriage they were riding in.

She and Peggy were accompanied by the newly betrothed couple Miss Alcott and Mr. Foster Northcott. Lord Merton's beautiful carriage was made for two, but he had restrained himself from taking Peggy along with him, merely following them as closely as the road allowed. Connie assumed Peggy was disappointed but too loyal to leave her side. It was heart-warming to say the least.

Some of the gossip Connie had allowed herself to overhear indicated that Merton had pursued Miss Alcott when they had first arrived at the house party, so it seemed to Connie that it was a testament to his devotion to Peggy that he would accompany them all that day.

Connie's curiosity finally allowed her to swallow her indignation for the time being. She had always wished she could see into the minds of other people. What were they all thinking? Why had Daisy and Foster accompanied her and Peggy? And was Lord Merton uncomfortable to be with the lady he had previously pursued and the one he seemed to currently pursue at the same time? And what was Mr. Northcott thinking about it all?

Her mind seethed with the questions, but she knew she couldn't actually ask them, much to her disappointment. Societal whims and expectations could be a pain in the backside most of the time, she acknowledged, even as she followed them, with a smile pinned to her face.

For a moment Connie allowed her gaze to wander to the other vehicles in their little convoy heading toward these ruins she still considered ridiculous. She hoped she would be able to at least appear to think differently once they arrived.

It had been a surprise to see Mr. Wagner climb into the same carriage as Lady Bathurst, Lady Isabelle, and Lady Alcott. Lord Bathurst had claimed an indisposition and had remained behind at Everleigh.

Connie wondered what the occupants of that carriage were talking about. She also wondered if Wagner might be shifting his pursuit to the very young debutante. A part of her would be hugely relieved but then she would worry for the girl.

"Are you well?" Peggy murmured the question low enough that the courting couple didn't seem to notice.

Connie smiled. "Why do you ask?"

"I know you, you goose."

Connie lifted a shoulder. She couldn't exactly bare her soul in front of the newly engaged couple who were still little more than strangers to her.

"Later," she whispered to Peggy who squeezed her arm and nodded.

"Of course." Peggy's warm smile was a bit of balm to her roiling emotions. It was soothing to know she had someone on her side. At least one. Even when it seemed as though everyone else was against her. She would miss her companion if things between Peggy and Lord Merton followed through.

Connie took herself to task. Peggy was surely not the only person in the entire world who cared about her, and it was foolish of her to allow herself to become melancholy. She couldn't dwell on Florent and the investigation taking place at Everleigh that was excluding her, despite her possible involvement by association.

"What do you know of Canada?" Connie asked Miss Alcott in an attempt to escape her own disquieted thoughts.

Miss Alcott's smile brightened the day as she looked at her fiancé and then back at Connie. "Very little, yet," she admitted. "But I'm looking forward to learning first-hand."

"Are you nervous about the crossing?"

"Of course," Daisy answered with a light laugh. "I've never been on anything other than a rowboat in a pond. I never even took a river barge, if you can imagine." The young woman shot another fond glance at her fiancé before turning and adding, "But I have been assured that there is nothing to fear." She paused for a moment. "What about you, Lady Constance? Have you ever crossed the ocean?"

"Not yet," she admitted, "But I have recently been thinking I ought to rectify that."

"Really?" Daisy demanded. "Would you go to Canada, too? Perhaps you could visit us," she offered eagerly.

Connie laughed, pleased with the invitation, but then she shook her head. "I don't think my adventurous spirit is quite that developed," she admitted. "From what I understand, Canada, especially Upper Canada where I believe you will be heading, isn't very developed yet. I think I might be better off exploring New York first."

Daisy stared and fidgeted, nerves flickering across her face for a moment before she resolutely nodded. "That is probably true. And as a woman on her own, you probably would be better served remaining where it's safer."

"Not to say New York is all that civilized for all its development," Mr. Northcott added with a chuckle. "You might be best attaching yourself to a more permanent travel companion before you venture across the Atlantic, just as my Daisy has done."

Connie gritted her teeth. Once more, marriage is seen as the solution to everything. But she had seen with her own sisters that it brought an entire passel of a different sort of trouble. More trouble than solutions, to Connie's way of thinking. One of her sisters thought marriage to a foreign prince was the perfect future but from the letters Connie received, her royal brother-in-law was an entitled bear to live with. Both of her sisters thought they were marrying for love. It did not recommend itself to Connie, that was for certain. Of course, she couldn't say that to the clearly in love newly engaged couple. She only hoped her smile carried a degree of sincerity as she offered it to them.

"What did you like best about New York when you were there, Mr. Northcott?"

"The vibrancy," he answered immediately. "For all its wildness that I worry would make it unsafe for a gentlewoman, there is a pulsing life to the city as it grows and accommodates such a vast variety of people. Far more so than our own London, even though our capital is much larger for now. I foresee that New York will thrive and grow to being a leader in the world. With ocean-going travel developing so quickly that you can cross the Atlantic in less than two months, I think more and more people will venture forth. Especially those in search of the new opportunities. That is where our capital fails. We are so stuck in our historic ways that it is hard for newcomers to make headway. In the new world, everyone except the natives are newcomers. It makes for a thrilling atmosphere."

Listening to him, for a moment, Connie was gripped with jealousy that he had already seen and experienced it and yet thought she oughtn't to do so. But, as he said, not necessarily applying to himself, everyone here was stuck in the old ways.

"Will you get to see New York while you're nearer?"

Connie tried very hard not to be jealous as the two newly betrothed exchanged another glance that seemed to speak an entire conversation in seconds. How could they be so in tune with one another when they'd only just become betrothed? Connie's stomach clenched as she reminded herself that she didn't want to belong to any man and the only way to maintain her full independence was to remain single. She wasn't jealous of the other young lady, she insisted to herself as she awaited their answer.

"We aren't certain," Daisy began almost haltingly. "A part of me would really like to see it for myself. But even though we'll be nearer from one perspective in that there will no longer be an ocean between us, it's still a very long way from where we will be in Upper Canada to New York. And there aren't necessarily roads or anything that might make travel easier."

"The easiest way is by river, to be honest. And the river will freeze at some point." Mr. Foster Northcott had started his explanation before another glance was exchanged between them and then to her surprise colour tinged his cheeks. "It might work out to go there by the springtime, but if we become in an interesting condition, we might have to decide between remaining in the colonies or coming home."

Connie's eyes widened and she had to again remind herself that this was not what she wanted for herself. Even though they sounded like they were setting out on the best adventure, it wasn't what she wanted for herself. Perhaps if she repeated it enough times within the confines of her mind, she would believe it.

"Are you nervous about the primitive conditions, Miss Alcott?"

Daisy grinned. "Of course," she said immediately. "Which is why New York would hold a certain appeal. But I do want to see for myself what Foster, I mean Mr. Northcott, has been up to these past years."

Connie smiled even as her stomach further curdled. They shouldn't have elected to join the doting couple for this drive. Turning to Peggy, Connie took in her companion's expression and knew the poor dear was longing for the same understanding for herself.

And in that moment, Connie couldn't even blame her. Being in perfect harmony with another person sounded perfectly lovely. If it could be guaranteed, everyone would surely want that for themselves. But Connie knew with certainty that there were no guarantees in life. Just take her own sisters. They were each wed to gentlemen they had thought they were head over toes in love with. They had chosen carefully, or so they had thought. One sister was wed to a foreign prince who had sunk in melancholy over the fact that he could not return to his country. That had been a surprising development as Connie's sister had thought the gentleman had been content to make England his home. She had no interest in returning to his small principality so far from her own family. So, it was not a cozy union for them.

Connie's other sister had chosen to wed a wealthy businessman who was not high ton. She was happier in some ways, but it was very uncomfortable for her that her husband wasn't accepted everywhere. It would be even more difficult when their children were grown, Connie was sure. Would they be gentry or commoners? Would Society accept or reject the poor dears. At present, it was impossible to imagine anyone rejecting the little urchins. But urchins grew up and would have to make their own way. It would be easier for the daughters, Connie was sure. Family could sponsor them. And they were sure to have generous dowries that would make them even more acceptable. But they would end up being an even more divided family if that happened, especially if Connie's nephews were not to be accepted by Society.

Society was ridiculous, Connie thought vehemently. All the more reason to set out on another adventure, far from the strictures of English High Society. But it was what she had been born to and it was uncomfortable to wish to leave it behind. Not that she truly wished to do so. She was so torn in her thoughts. And the rejection she had felt from Florent Alcott had only jumbled her feelings further.

She needed to find out what Henry Wagner was doing at Everleigh. If he was tied into the reason for the Agents being there, then it might develop that he could be arrested and deported, and she need never concern herself with his presence again. The thought enticed her. Should she ask Mr. Northcott about him? Connie tapped her chin, wondering how she might bring it up.

"I suppose you already knew everyone who was invited to this party before your arrival, Miss Alcott?"

The young woman across from her smiled and nodded. "I did, yes." She agreed, before a slight hesitation. "Well, for the most part, anyway. Did you? I know you've been travelling extensively for years. But you made your debut before you went abroad, didn't you?"

"I did make my debut, but there were several people I hadn't encountered in my brief time being fully active in Society." Connie paused, debating if she ought to broach the subject, but then she decided to carry forth. "What about you, Mr. Northcott? You've also been abroad for quite some time, haven't you? Was everyone strangers for you or were they all familiar?"

"I'm in a similar situation as you, my lady. Some were familiar and others much less so."

"Do you enjoy making new acquaintances?" she asked, less specifically, more of a broad question.

Mr. Northcott shrugged and shook his head slightly. "Yes and no," he answered with a laugh. "It is often interesting and beneficial to meet new people. But it isn't necessarily one of my favorite things, I'll admit." He laughed lightly and then looked directly at Connie. "You must love meeting new people, I suppose, with your travels, you must be forever encountering new people."

Connie nodded slowly. "Some are delightful," she agreed. "Others less so," she added with a laugh. "And while abroad, the circles can often be even smaller than amongst the ton during the Season, if you can imagine. Or perhaps you are aware. I would imagine there aren't a great number of people near you in Upper Canada."

"You are correct. My closest neighbours are quite distant, aside from my crew that are right on my property."

Connie nodded. Then, finally, taking her courage in both hands, she tried not to betray her nerves and hoped she appeared nonchalant when she finally stated, "I was surprised to see Mr. Wagner here. Have you been long acquainted?"

Her gaze was watchful despite her desire to hide her interest, so she caught the flicker of surprise and disgust that crossed Mr. Northcott's face before he smoothed his expression into one of mild interest. "Are you acquainted with the man, then?" he asked without answering her question. But she supposed his evasiveness was an answer in itself from a certain standpoint.

"We have met, yes. As I said, I was surprised to encounter him in Everleigh." Connie had hoped to gain information, not find herself on the side of being questioned.

"Why were you surprised by his presence here?" Connie thought she saw cunning speculation in Mr. Northcott's eyes and tried not to bristle under it.

"I am unsure how to put this politely," she began with what she hoped was a hesitant smile. "He has been persistent in his efforts to pursue a courtship with me. A courtship I do not welcome."

"Ah, I see, then that would have been a most unwelcome surprise, in that case," Mr. Northcott replied mildly with a gentle smile that encompassed all in the carriage. His fiancé was gazing at him with a slightly puzzled expression, but he didn't address her. "I must apologize on behalf of my family for making you uncomfortable, Lady Constance. I wasn't expecting to see him here either, to be frank. I thought Lady Adelaide was a little higher in the instep than to have one such as he at her quite exclusive entertainment, but there we have it, we all must endure the vagaries of being someone's guest."

"I had never met him," Miss Alcott jumped into the conversation. "But I was surprised, too, because I was under the impression that Lady Adelaide had told me about everyone who was to attend."

"So, you knew I'd be here, then," Mr. Northcott teased her. "Were you hoping to entrap me, my dear?"

"This is not the point of our current conversation, sir," Miss Alcott protested, blushing. "We are discussing Mr. Wagner, not you." She turned back to Connie. "I'm sorry that he is bothering you, can we help in any way? I didn't get a wonderful first impression of him, which is why I was surprised my friends included him here. How can we help?"

Connie was touched by her offer but wasn't certain how to answer her. Thus far she had done a rather excellent job of protecting herself, she thought. But his arrival had given her a bad feeling. And sharing the burden would be such a relief. On the other hand, she didn't actually know these people well, and trusting others wasn't her strong suit. Besides, Miss Alcott's brother had practically accused her of somehow being involved with a scheme involving Henry Wagner, so she shouldn't be so very appeased by his sister's kindness.

"I truly appreciate the offer and perhaps I'll take you up on it but at this point, I have no idea what I might need. For now, Miss Smith has been doing her best to ensure I don't find myself forced into an uncomfortable situation."

"Oh, no, how dreadful that would be. We shall do our part to share in that, as well," Miss Alcott immediately replied. Connie grinned when the young woman's new fiancé quickly nodded his agreement to the scheme.

"You are all being very kind."

"That man gave me the shivers when I first laid eyes upon him. I couldn't have even told you why at the time. So, it will not be a hardship in the very least to put a spoke in his wheels, I can assure you."

For the first time since returning from the continent, perhaps even for the first time in years before that,

Constance Moreland felt a sense of homecoming. There were nice people being kind to her, not for anything they might gain from it, merely for the fact that they wished to be friends.

In that moment, she forgot about all the negative things that had been swirling within her that morning.

When they finally arrived at their destination, Connie made her way to Lady Adelaide's side as casually as she could muster and probed for information about the investigation. They hadn't been able to find out much the night before, and Connie was determined to find out what she could from her noble hostess.

"I do apologize, my lady," Lady Adelaide said in a low but urgent voice. "I know you wanted to be involved and I tried every wile I could think of to convince my husband to bring us with them."

Connie's breath hitched. "Bring us with them where?"

Lady Adelaide glanced around in an almost dramatic way making Connie giggle despite the anger she was struggling to control. She felt as though she were directly involved in this situation, and it infuriated her to be left out and in the dark.

"You mustn't tell anyone," Lady Adelaide said firmly.

"Of course not," Connie tried not to be offended.

"They, that is, Adelaide, his brother Gilbert who just arrived with the agents, and Mr. Alcott, as well as the agents, of course, have gone to the beach where the cotton was found. They want to find out what they can about where they are coming from and who is involved."

"I see." Connie didn't actually see. But she didn't know what else to say. "Do they have any suspicions about who might be connected?"

"There is some fear that it is some of our tenants." Lady Adelaide sounded both mournful and offended, making Connie again fight against inappropriate humour.

"What about any of your guests?" Connie asked the question despite the possibility of it causing offense.

Lady Adelaide was far from stupid, despite her seeming preoccupation with certain things Connie might consider silly. She grew still and stared at Connie with a shrewd gaze.

"Did you have anyone in particular in mind?"

Connie pursed her lips and sighed through her nose. *Ought she to say what she was really thinking?*

"I was surprised to find Mr. Wagner as a fellow guest," she commented, seemingly apropos of nothing. Lady Adelaide smiled and nodded.

"It was curious, was it not? I wasn't sure if it would delight or offend you, and I do apologize if you have been made uncomfortable." She paused and again glanced around, this time far more discretely. "Excuse me for saying this, but again, I must ask that you refrain from repeating what I'm about to tell you." Connie nodded despite her irritation. "Mr. Wagner was invited at the request of my brother-in-law."

Connie frowned. "That's odd. Which one?"

"Gilbert. And yes, it was a trifle odd. I am pleased that Foster and Daisy were able to become betrothed despite all these irregularities. And if I'm not mistaken, there might be another happy event to celebrate," Lady Adelaide said with a suggestive twinkle in her eye.

"Yes, yes, of course, but what about Wagner?"

Lady Adelaide shrugged. "He hasn't been much trouble despite no one really seeming to like the man very much. It's a mere minor inconvenience as far as I can tell."

Connie opened her mouth as though to object but managed to swallow back her thoughts before they came out of her mouth.

"Yes, of course, but do you think there's a possibility Wagner might be involved in some way with the other situation?"

"I think it's possible, but I have been forbidden from asking him directly."

Connie had to laugh. "Would that be your first impulse, then?"

"I'm afraid it might have been. I do like to get straight to the heart of a matter if I can."

"I can respect that," Connie said. "But if it was your husband who did the forbidding, I can fully understand why he might have done so."

Lady Adelaide laughed and nodded. "As can I, after further reflection. I am still wretchedly sorry for you that we couldn't accompany the gentlemen."

"Did your husband by any chance say anything about Mr. Wagner?"

"Only that I was to be careful of him."

"Did you understand that advice? Careful of him how? Such as, keep an eye on him, or don't hurt his feelings?"

Lady Adelaide laughed again. "You are delightfully amusing, my lady. I strongly doubt my husband was overly concerned about the man's feelings."

Connie nodded. "Do you suppose we ought to follow him?"

"I have my other guests to think about so I cannot assist you in this, but if you do try to find out anything about the man, do be careful. I would hate to think you had gotten into trouble due to my inattention."

"I shall be perfectly fine," Connie soothed even as she turned her attention elsewhere. Peggy was nowhere to be seen at the moment, but Connie saw that Mr. Wagner was strolling about nearby, his shifty gaze seemingly everywhere at once.

She spent the rest of their time at the ruins trying to be as unobtrusive as possible while she also kept a close eye on whomever Wagner spoke with.

Chapter Sixteen

Connie was vacillating between misery and delight. She was trying very hard not to be consumed with jealousy as she watched her friend and companion become affianced to Viscount Merton. But her stomach was beginning to cramp from the effort. Lady Adelaide was evidently not divided in her affections. She was thrilled by the coup that was her house party. Two betrothals in a week. The viscountess would be crowned the most successful hostess at her very first effort. From the corner of her eye, Connie could see her ladyship trying valiantly not to crow with delight.

Merton had at least had the sense not to propose to Peggy in front of everyone but had done so quickly and privately before returning to the group milling about the ruins, both of them wreathed in smiles that could not be hidden.

Everyone had immediately congratulated the pair even while some of the other young women had cast Peggy jealous glances, prompting Connie to step forward and offer her full support to her impoverished relative. While she might be a little envious of her companion's happiness, she didn't actually begrudge it to her and could not allow anyone to dampen it.

But now Connie would be forced to make decisions she didn't want to face. Even though she had suspected this might be the direction things would go, now that it was upon her and her companion was truly going to leave her, Connie was dreading all the changes.

And this on top of the accusatory expression in the handsome Mr. Alcott's eyes that morning over breakfast, it was a wonder she had been able to keep the contents of her stomach settled as well as she had. Not to say that her insides were at all settled, but at least she had managed not to share them with the others.

She couldn't even enjoy the likely quite delightful remnants of the ancient building left by some long ago Northcott ancestors. Under usual circumstances, Connie quite delighted in exploring old ruins but today their charm was completely lost on her. All she wanted to do was curl up in some corner on a comfortable chair with a soft cat and a good book and escape from her troubles for a couple of hours. Just enough to get some distance from her raw feelings of abandonment.

Connie called herself to task. No one was abandoning her. Mr. Alcott didn't owe her any sort of loyalty. The fact that she had inexplicably developed warm and trusting feelings toward him did not obligate him in any way toward her. And he really hadn't harmed her in any way. At least not physically. The fact that he suspected her of involvement in the smuggling was ludicrous and would be proven wrong in short order. It should also make his suspicions no longer hurtful because he was clearly not of sound mind so she shouldn't care what he thought of her. But her heart was a stubborn organ and wouldn't listen to her mind.

Peggy was also not abandoning her, Connie reminded herself. She had never made a secret of the fact that she wished for marriage. It was part of why Connie had agreed to attend the house party. They had both understood it was a possibility. And Connie was happy for the woman, she insisted. But she was sad for herself and bereft of where that might leave her in the future.

But she was being a selfish beast. And so, she smiled pleasantly as she was handed up into the carriage she had arrived in, this time, the return to Everleigh would be a much lighter ride. Peggy was to accompany Lord Merton in his fine high carriage and Mr. Foster Northcott had elected to ride one of the horses the grooms had brought for just that sort of eventuality.

"How cozy it will be with just the two of us," Miss Alcott had enthused when she was handed in after Connie.

Connie was proud to note that her smile didn't waver over her travel companion's words. But really the last place she wished to be was holed up in a closed carriage with Florent Alcott's sister.

"Tell me what you think of my brother," Daisy ordered as soon as their carriage began rolling. Connie grabbed the strap by her head both to steady herself from the sudden movement and to steady her nerves to endure the conversation.

"He seems to be a pleasant fellow."

"Damned by faint praise," Daisy crowed, seemingly delighted by the response. "He would be devasted were he to hear you."

"No, why would he?" Connie asked, hoping she sounded barely interested.

"I think you caught his eye."

"Not for the reasons you might think," Connie countered. "He seems to be labouring under the misapprehension that I am involved with Mr. Wagner."

"Never say so. He isn't that stupid."

"He actually said as much to me over breakfast this morning."

That silenced Daisy as she sat back in her seat, stunned at the thought of her brother's misinformation.

A few moments later she rallied.

"We will just have to set him straight, in that case."

"Do not trouble yourself on my account, my dear Miss Alcott. You have your own future to see to, you needn't spare anyone else's a thought at this time."

"It's no trouble at all," Daisy waved away Connie's words. "I have always thought Florent one of the best fellows I know. I would like to see him happy."

Connie's throat tightened at the kind words the other woman had for her brother. Uninterested in sinking into melancholy, Connie struck up a rather inane conversation that kept them preoccupied for several minutes. And so, they didn't notice the commotion outside their carriage until they were already moving quicker and starting to bounce over a rougher road.

"Whatever is happening?" Daisy demanded as she and Connie exchanged questioning looks. Connie once more grabbed hold of the strap by her head, this time to steady herself as she stood in the swaying carriage so that she could reach to pound on the roof.

Her clear demand to stop was evidently ignored by their driver. The occupants of the carriage again exchanged looks, but this time they were filled with more than questions.

"Hold on tight, Daisy," Connie called out to her friend as she peered through the window trying to see what might be going on. Did she dare to open the window and stick her head out to get a better idea what was happening? At this speed, it might not be safe. But she wasn't sure if she could bear to just sit quietly.

With a sudden jolt that would have sent them both to the floor if they weren't holding on, their carriage came to a lurching stop, and the wild ride was over as abruptly as it had begun. Connie couldn't even fathom how much time had passed. It had felt like an eon had passed while the carriage had bounded over bumps and ruts in the road, but it was possible that it hadn't been nearly as long as it had felt.

She was just reaching for the door when it was yanked open from the outside. Somehow, she wasn't even surprised to see Henry Wagner standing there.

"Time to get out, you two," he demanded. Connie thought he was there for her. He looked dangerous and she had to swallow her fear, but she couldn't allow him to hurt her friend.

"Leave her out of this, Mr. Wagner," she demanded as she stepped closer to the open door.

"No such luck. It's not you I want this time," he sneered. "Your usefulness has been replaced by hers," he continued.

A wave of relief crashed over her, quickly followed by confusion. "Whatever do you mean? What do you want with us?"

"I wanted your money, but now I will have to make do with keeping my neck out of a noose. And for that, this one will be much more helpful."

"What are you talking about?" Connie demanded.

Daisy must have been briefly stunned into silence but her uncharacteristic quiet came to an end. "I'm not going anywhere with you," she said haughtily, not budging from her seat.

"Get down and make it quick," Wagner snarled. "I'll shoot this pretty lady straight away if you don't hurry and do as I say."

Connie swallowed the bile that threatened and tried not to appear as terrified as she felt when Wagner pulled a gun out of the waistband of his pants.

"You could have just asked politely." Daisy sneered as she reluctantly did as he demanded, stepping in front of Connie and through the open door.

Both girls fought their fear as they surveyed the scene that confronted them when they stepped down from the leaning carriage. It seemed they had narrowly avoided overturning in a ditch when the carriage had been brought to such a sudden stop.

Mr. Wagner's valet had his gun trained upon the carriage driver from where he sat on a large horse. He had another two horses tied to his saddle horn while what was obviously Mr. Wagner's mount waited patiently for his rider.

"What is the meaning of this?" Connie demanded, sounding far braver than she felt.

"I've got no time for you and your infernal questions," Mr. Wagner growled. "I'm in a hurry. Mount up or I'll put a bullet through you. While I'd still happily wed your inheritance, I'll get rid of you if you are going to be more trouble than you're worth."

"But what do you need with Miss Alcott?" Connie was more than confused.

"She is even better insurance than you are at this point since it's her fiancé who has become much too suspicious of me for my comfort. And it's not going to take him long to notice we turned off from following the other carriages. Hurry." He was shouting by the time he got to the end of his speech. Wagner's frenzied gaze stared over the women's shoulders. "Hurry, we've got to get moving."

Rather than obey his imperative, Daisy and Connie followed his gaze with their own. They could all see the cloud of dust off in the distance. It would seem pursuit had already begun.

~~~~

Florent had known something was wrong even before he set out. There was a dull ache deep in his bones. He didn't know what it meant and worried it was something to do with his mother, but when he encountered the train of Lady Adelaide and her guests heading back to Everleigh, he found his mother happily ensconced with her friends.

"Where's my sister?" he demanded of Foster, who was riding post at the front of the convoy.

With a few choice words it became evident that the carriage with Daisy and Connie in it was missing. In moments, the rest of the guests carried on while Foster, Florent, and a gang of grooms turned back to investigate.

"Wagner isn't here, either," Foster said to Florent when they were away from the others.

"I noticed," Florent said without further comment.

Panic settled low in his belly as they began the search for the missing women. Florent was thankful on one hand that he knew the area so well. But knowing all the roads and byways also meant that he was well aware of how many places there might be to hide if one was inclined to do so.

Before he could despair, though, they caught sight of the missing carriage off in the distance and galloped toward it with little heed for any possible danger.

The carriage was empty of its occupants with only the coachman tied up and unconscious beside the left front wheel. They saw the man was still breathing, but they doubted they would get many answers from him. Leaving one groom behind to see to the older servant, they set off in pursuit. They could tell from the
~~~~

hoofprints that several horses had recently left, and the answers they sought would not be found in the empty carriage.

Thankfully, within minutes, they saw their quarry off in the distance and once more they urged their horses into a neck or nothing pace.

As they neared, Florent's heart lodged itself in his throat when he realized that both Connie and Daisy had their wrists tied together while Wagner and his henchman were leading their horses at a reckless pace. Suddenly, though he didn't see how she managed it, Connie tugged her horse's lead out of the valet's seemingly inattentive grasp and urged the horse away from the cluster of horses.

Confusion followed and Florent almost lost sight of what was taking place, wishing he could have his gaze divided between what was happening with his sister, who was held firmly in Wagner's grasp, and Connie being pursued by the henchman.

Florent's heartbeat sped up and then nearly stopped as Foster raised his gun and took aim. Foster's most excellent marksmanship had managed to shoot the gun out of Wagner's hand without either the criminal nor Daisy getting hurt in the process, leaving Florent free to urge his horse even faster after the fleeing Constance and her pursuer. It all happened very fast. More action than Florent had ever before experienced, and it made him realize he had been lacking any sort of adventure in his life. It was an errant thought that he fought to dismiss even as he was in hot pursuit.

So preoccupied with chasing Connie was the clearly not so bright valet that he didn't realize how close Florent was when he leaned over and shoved him from his saddle. The valet's pursuit was over that quickly, but Connie didn't respond to his calls to halt.

Florent's horse was more powerful than the one Connie was on and within moments, Flor was able to overtake her and bring her to a stop. Nearly beside herself, Connie fought him briefly before she realized who had caught her when Florent jumped down and pulled her from the back of the horse.

It was all madness, but the urgency of the matter made reaction settle in, and Florent pulled Connie into his arms for a quick embrace before he allowed his hands to travel over her to ascertain if she had been injured. Connie stiffened suddenly and their eyes met. Florent's face hovered near hers for a moment as he briefly contemplated kissing her senseless.

His intention must have shown itself in his face for she quickly looked away and raised her still-tied hands between them.

"I do thank you for the assistance, Mr. Alcott. Would you be so kind as to untie me?"

Despite the multitude of emotions flowing through him, he couldn't help the grin that nearly split his face. She was right to prevent his ardor. Now was certainly not the time. He got her untied and back on the horse in time for them to turn back and watch Daisy and Foster handily deal with Wagner while a couple of grooms wrestled Wagner's valet into a trussed-up position on his horse with the very ropes he had used to tie Connie.

"What is the meaning of this?" Wagner was yelling loudly. Even from the distance where they were, they could hear him clearly. "You cannot treat me this way."

"You're lucky I only shot the gun out of your hand, you imbecile. With the way you were brandishing it at my betrothed, I was tempted to put the bullet through your heart."

Florent had to avert his gaze as his sister threw herself into Foster's arms. There were some things a brother should never witness. To his shock but secret delight, Connie giggled from where she rode at his side. Clearly the young woman was made of sterner stuff than he would have ever suspected. She ought to be in hysterics from the ordeal she had just been through. Florent was inordinately proud of her for no reason that he could have explained. Or rather, he could have explained in great detail why she was worthy of pride, he just couldn't say why he was in a position to feel said pride toward the woman.

It was a mixed cloud of confusion and triumph in which they rode back to Everleigh with Foster calmly explaining to Wagner and his valet just which ship he planned to have them sent upon to serve their sentences in a penal colony for their involvement in the smuggling ring.

"I had nothing to do with it," Wagner kept shouting, which would be immediately followed by his valet's equally vehement insistence that it had all been Wagner's idea.

Chapter Seventeen

Constance stood by the window in the small salon she was hiding in. She would never have thought of herself as the sort to hide, but there was no other explanation for what she was doing. There was too much love floating in the air, and she could barely stomach it.

That also made her feel dreadful.

She was happy for the betrothed couples, she truly was. And perhaps if she repeated the words to herself often enough, she would believe them.

Connie hoped she had said all the right things to Peggy when that good woman giggled out her news. The giggles had felt very out of character to Connie and had set her teeth on edge, but she supposed any woman who had just been proposed to by a handsome viscount might be prone to a giggle or two. Not that Connie had any desire to become betrothed to a viscount handsome or otherwise, she insisted to herself and refused to allow her mind to linger on one particular heir to a viscountcy.

"Lady Constance?"

Her efforts not to think about him must have conjured him, she thought a little wildly as she turned from the window slowly, trying to swallow all reactions before she faced him.

"Mr. Alcott," she replied with little inflection, offering him a slight bow.

"Could I please have a moment of your time?"

"I have nothing else to do at the moment," she conceded, ignoring how very ungracious she sounded. She found it harder to ignore how handsome he looked when his cheek stretched into a half smile as though he couldn't decide whether or not to be amused over her churlishness. Even though she hated to think he might laugh at her, she was feeling too miserable to muster any anger.

"Perhaps we might sit over here?" Florent asked, indicating the small alcove to the side; the two comfortable chairs appeared to be the coziest spot in the large, imposing estate. Connie fought against being charmed. She wasn't finished wallowing in her misery. But it was challenging when his lopsided smile barely wavered despite her refusal to return it.

Connie forced herself to look past the end of her nose and her own confused feelings and really look at the man before her. She couldn't actually fathom what he might wish to discuss with her but getting out of her own melancholy, she could see that he was nervous. She didn't think it had to do with her, but since she was the only one in the room, she had an inkling that it might. A flutter began in the center of her being that she couldn't decide if it was a good sensation or not.

Perhaps he was going to rebuke her once more. But if so, would he look nervous? She was no longer sure of anything. Her entire life felt topsy turvy after Peggy and Merton's sudden betrothal. Even though she had thought she had prepared herself for the possible outcome, she clearly hadn't done so.

She was woolgathering and Connie called herself to account and followed Florent's lead, perching herself delicately on the edge of the chair he had indicated, feeling the need to be prepared for taking immediate flight should she feel inclined.

It took effort, but Connie tried not to flutter. Nerves coursed through her, and every limb wanted to fidget. Her hands clasped each other tightly and she placed them firmly in her lap, training her gaze to the gentleman's face and admonishing her eyes not to faulter.

After clearing his throat a time or two, to her amazement, Florent actually reached up and tugged on the circle of the collar of his shirt as though it were too tight or he was not getting sufficient air. That further evidence of his nerves helped to settle her own and she sat back a little further onto her chair, not quite relaxing but a little less urged to flee.

"Thank you for sitting with me," Florent finally began after another silent moment passed between them. "I do trust I didn't interrupt you. You appeared quite pensive at the window."

Connie shrugged. "I was pensive. I have much to ponder."

Florent nodded. "I suppose the imminent marriage of your companion might put a damper on your own plans."

"I cannot travel alone, unfortunately," Connie agreed.

"And is traveling the only occupation you can envision for your life?"

Connie's gaze sharpened onto his. What an odd question. She opened her mouth to reply but didn't actually know what to say and so shut it with a snap.

"I didn't mean to be impertinent," Florent excused.

"It wasn't necessarily impertinent," Connie allowed. "I just don't have an answer to your question. What else would you have me do? I have considered settling into a cottage by the sea and having cats, but I will still require a companion for that. My family cannot countenance my being alone."

"Have you thought of returning to live with your family?"

"I cannot countenance that," she replied immediately but softened her seeming rebuke with a smile. "As time will march on, I would have to be someone's dependent. It will not be my home. Already it isn't, but if my parents were to pass and my brother marries, surely it will be all the less comfortable for me. I need to make a home for myself or continue my travels. There isn't much other choice for a woman, especially not a noblewoman."

"Seems to me a noblewoman has more choice than others. Certainly, more than a nobleman."

Connie was taken aback by his words. "Do you truly feel as though you have no choices?" She was shocked, and her surprise seemed to amuse the gentleman.

"As the heir, what would you have me do?"

"Ah, I see what you mean." Connie nodded. "But did you never think to at least have your Grand Tour? Live a little before taking on the mantle of responsibility?"

"That mantle was thrust upon me before I had a chance to consider other options."

Connie frowned, not fully understanding but didn't feel herself free to ask for further clarification.

"Would you feel completely constrained in your cottage by the sea after your years of travel?"

"Constrained? I'm not certain. I think it sounds rather heavenly, as I could make it perfectly how I'd wish. No more different beds or noisy inns."

Suddenly Florent appeared eager to hear more. Connie had noticed his rapt attention whenever she had spoken of her travels, but now he seemed delighted to hear it hadn't all been delightful either.

"So, staying in one place might appeal to you?"

Connie lifted her shoulder in a rather helpless shrug. "I think it really might. But as I said, my family insists I must be accompanied, and that complicates matters."

There was a moment of silence while Connie had the impression Florent was trying to search her soul through her eyes. She wanted desperately to look away but found herself unable to do so.

"You could marry," he finally said.

"That would be a rather drastic conclusion to what ought to be an easy problem to solve."

"Would it be so terrible?" He was back to looking bashful and nervous, and Connie sternly told her heart it was not allowed to melt.

"It could be," she finally answered. "There have thus far only rather dastardly oafs applying for the position." Connie found it almost impossible to keep her voice light and her expression unconcerned but was startled when Florent finally reached out and claimed her hands from where they were clasped in her lap.

"I swear I would try most valiantly not to be of the dastardly sort," Florent vowed in a strained voice while Connie could only blink at him in surprise.

"What are you saying, Mr. Alcott?" Her voice was barely above a whisper, and she couldn't even swallow as her mouth had gone dry.

"I'm saying that while I know you might not have any desire to forgive me and it would be a rather dull reduction in your circumstances to wed with a provincial gentleman such as myself, but that you would at least have the consolation of making me the happiest man in all of Christendom."

Connie stared at him without even blinking before a burble of laughter fought its way from her throat.

"That was too convoluted by far. Please explain yourself, sir." Connie tried to sound as though she were reprimanding him, but she couldn't bring herself to pull her hands from his grasp. Suddenly the day appeared delightful, and she thought she could sit in that very spot for the rest of her life.

Florent must have sensed her relenting as he appeared to relax right before her eyes. But his gaze sharpened and his grasp on her hands tightened as he leaned toward her even more earnestly.

"What I mean to say, my lady, my dear Constance, is that if you are willing to consider a cottage by the sea, perhaps you might also see the possibilities of an estate by the river. And I'm almost certain your family would consider me to be an acceptable companion to guard the proprieties."

Another gurgle of laughter escaped Constance. "You are quite correct in that regard, Mr. Alcott. My family would find you nearly perfect."

"Only nearly?" he asked with a quirk of his eyebrow.

She shrugged. "You aren't heir to a dukedom, now are you?"

They laughed together before sobering.

"Would you consider it, though, Constance? I know the country life might appear dull after the adventures you had. And I cannot even begin to reminisce with you as I've barely been anywhere. But I would allow you carte blanche of my estate, and I think you might find it a different sort of adventure and might be quite to your taste."

"I might consider it, possibly," Connie admitted, "but you must tell me if you would ever see your way clear to doing any travelling at all."

"I've always wanted to, but I've been too burdened with turning around the Alcott fortunes for the past decade. And then it seemed as though the opportunity had passed me by."

"I see," Connie replied, her heart wanting to soar. She just might be going to find what she had been secretly hoping for all along. He wasn't making the sort of declaration that it seemed Mr. Northcott and Lord Merton had made to their new fiancés, but Connie might allow herself to be contented with the arrangement anyway. She would at least be safe from the likes of fortune hunters such as the Henry Wagners of the world.

"I'm not sure if I feel brave enough to promise you we could venture to the new world, but I would certainly vow to leave the estate from time to time."

Connie took a deep breath and dared to look him in the eye as she asked her next question. "And what exactly makes you think that we would suit? It was just a day ago that you were on the verge of accusing me of being in league with Mr. Wagner and the smugglers."

"To my utter shame, you are right. But you see, it's because I was falling in love with you and didn't know what to do with my feelings."

Connie blinked and her jaw dropped open in shock. "Are you jesting with me?" she demanded before softening quickly. "No, of course you wouldn't jest about something like that but –" she trailed off, unsure how to complete her sentence.

"Is my declaration too sudden for you? Does it make my proposal more or less appealing?"

Connie stared at him, still unsure how to answer or what to say. "I don't actually recall hearing a proposal, Mr. Alcott," she finally said primly, feeling laughter wanting to bubble from her.

"That was most remiss of me, I do apologize," Florent replied immediately, standing, and offering her an elegant bow before dropping to his knee and reaching out for her hand once more. Connie was still so muddled by the turn of events she didn't resist when he separated her hands from their grip on one another and brought one of them to his lips, dropping a kiss onto the back of it and keeping a firm hold lest she try to escape.

"Lady Constance Moreland, I find I love you quite desperately despite our short acquaintance. Would you do me the great honor of agreeing to be my wife?"

Tears sprang to her eyes. It was the most perfect thing he could have said to her. "The pleasure would be mine," she answered simply.

With that, he closed the distance that separated their faces and finally answered the questions they had both been having since that almost kiss the day before.

Epilogue

Lady Adelaide was sipping tea in her husband's library reading her correspondence and rubbing her growing belly.

"There seems to be no end to the entreaties from any and all Society mothers asking that I host them and their daughters at my next house party."

"You do not sound pleased," her fond husband commented, pausing in the perusal of his own pile of letters.

Amelia sighed. "You might think it's daft, but my first foray into hostess duty was much too successful. I'll never be able to replicate it. Three betrothals in a week? What a coup! But the expectations it has raised are unattainable and unnatural. All these mothers think I have some sort of magical gift."

Lucian smiled at his much-loved wife. "You do, I can assure you of that."

Amelia laughed and blushed but waved away his words. "I'm happy to read that Daisy and Foster made it safely across the vast Atlantic. I will admit to you that I was thrilled for Daisy's happiness but terrified about her future."

"My brother will take excellent care of your friend."

"I don't doubt he'll do his best, but can you truly say he's a match for an ocean?"

Lucian laughed but answered proudly, "He *is* a Northcott."

Amelia rolled her eyes before glancing back at the sheaf of papers in her hand. "The soon to be Lady Merton has much news. Connie's family has been driving themselves to distraction dividing themselves between Peggy and Connie, doing their best to arrange everyone's lives just how they think best. Thankfully both ladies seem capable of ignoring their directives. I do believe both of those couples will do quite well."

"Are you happy about your newest neighbour, then?"

"Quite," Amelia answered with a firm nod.

"I'm left to sense some disappointment, though," Lucian commented.

Amelia sighed again. "Well, I am happy that Lord Merton found his match. And I'm thrilled that Daisy is so happy with Foster. But surely you know that I had both Lord Merton and Lord Simmons in mind as possible matches for Daisy. I was almost certain she would choose one of them."

"But as you said, you are happy with the matches that were arranged."

"I am, but as it turns out, it had really nothing to do with me, so all these mothers asking me for help are placing their hopes in a basket with a very large hole in it."

Lucian laughed at her metaphor but continued to watch her expectantly knowing there was more to her disquiet. Amelia sighed once more.

"To be honest, it's Lord Simmons I'm concerned about. If ever there was a man in need of a wife, I think it's him. There is something almost desolate about the man. I thought Daisy's cheerful soul would be an excellent counterbalance for the man, and vice versa."

Lucian waited while Amelia tapped her finger on her chin as she tended to do when deep in thought.

"Can I tell you something else?"

"Please do," he answered with a grin.

"I'm afraid Lord and Lady Bathurst might have set their sights on him. I thought their daughter, Lady

Isabelle was a delightfully sweet young woman, but there was something slightly shifty about her parents. I would hate to think there were more plots arising from my little party."

"My dear woman," Lucian began as he got up from behind his desk and pulled his wife out of her chair and into his arms. "You are worrying too much, which cannot be good for your condition. Lord Simmons is a grown man who can look after his own melancholy and watch out for any possible schemers. I don't know him exceptionally well, but I can assure you he is more than capable. Be happy about the three matches you made, especially your new sister-in-law. Considering you were most hopeful that Daisy would find a match, you ought to be delighted with that outcome."

Amelia snuggled herself into her husband's chest. "Oh, I am, have no fear about that. But can you imagine how stupendous it would have been had I arranged four matches?

Lucian shook his head and chuckled, leading his lady from the room.

The End

Want to find out what happens with Lord Simmons?
Read the next book in the *Northcott Kinship* series:

Provoking Lord Simmons

She was just trying to help another lady out...

The *Northcott Kinship* series is connected to the *Sherton Sisters*.

Have you read those yet?
Start with Book 1

A Duke to Elude

She's waiting for true love. He's tasked with uncovering the truth. When nefarious schemes threaten her reputation, he finds his heart on the line with it.

About the Author

I learned to read when I was four or five, listening to my mother read to me when I was lonely after my brother started school. Ever since, I've had my head buried in books. I love words – historical plaques, signs, the cereal box – but my first love has always been novels.

A little over ten years ago my husband dared me to write a book instead of always reading them. I didn't think I'd be able to do it, but to my surprise I love writing. Those early efforts eventually became my first published book – Tempting the Earl (published by Avalon Books in 2010). It has been a thrilling adventure as I learned to navigate the world of publishing.

I believe firmly that everyone deserves a happily ever after. I want my readers to be able to escape from the everyday for a little while and feel upbeat and refreshed when they get to the end of my books.

When not reading or writing, I can be found traipsing around my neighbourhood or travelling the world with my favourite companion.

Stay in touch:

Website Facebook Instagram Twitter

Stay in touch with Wendy May Andrews
and forthcoming publishing news.

Sign up for her biweekly newsletter

Other books by Wendy May Andrews:

Ladies of Mayfair

The Governess' Debut

The Debutante Bride

The Reluctant Debutante

Sweet Surrender

A Dangerous Debut

Mayfair Mayhem

The Duke Conspiracy

The Countess Intrigue

The Viscount Deception

The Bequest

Inheriting Trouble

Courting Intrigue

Inviting Misfortune

Sherton Sisters

A Duke to Elude

A Viscount to Conspire

A Lady to Reveal

A Gentleman to Avoid

A Sister to Beguile

Northcott Kinship

Assisting Lord Richmond

Evading the Gentleman

Intriguing Lord Adelaide

Distracting the Heir

Convincing Mr. Northcott

Provoking Lord Simmons

Orphan Train

Sophie

Katie

Cassie

Melanie

Married by Proxy

A Wife for Carter

A Wife for Alastair

A Wife for Ransom

A Wife for Hamilton

Dear Aunt Judy

Torn in Toronto

Singed in Saint John

Another breathtaking series you don't want to miss:
The Ladies of Mayfair - Book 1:

The Governess' Debut

The governess must charm both the spoiled child and the haughty earl.

Orphaned and destitute, gently born Felicia Scott must find a way to keep a roof over her head. No longer able to enter the Marriage Mart, but also not of the servant class, the only option is to find a position as governess.

After his spoiled, seven year old daughter has sent off three governesses in the 18 months since her mother died, the Earl of Standish doubts the young, inexperienced Miss Scott could possible manage the position. Since he's desperate and she comes so highly recommended, the earl agrees to give her a chance. Much to everyone's amazement, the beautiful, young governess succeeds where the others had failed. The entire household benefits from the calm, including the jaded earl.

How does he overcome his arrogance to see his governess' true value?

Available now on Amazon

If you like Regencies with a touch of adventure, you will love

the Mayfair Mayhem series. Book 1 is:

The Duke Conspiracy

Anything is possible with a spying debutante, a duke, and a conspiracy.

Growing up, Rose and Alex were the best of friends until their families became embroiled in a feud. Now, the Season is throwing them into each other's company. Despite the spark of attraction they might feel for one another, they each want very different things in life, besides needing to support their own family's side in the dispute.

Miss Rosamund Smythe is finding the Season to be a dead bore after spying with her father, a baron diplomat, in Vienna. She wants more out of life than just being some nobleman's wife. When she overhears a plot to entrap Alex into a marriage of convenience, her intrigue and some last vestige of loyalty causes them to overcome the feud.

His Grace, Alexander Milton, the Duke of Wrentham, wants a quiet life with a "proper" wife after his tumultuous childhood. His parents had fought viciously, lied often, and Alex had hated it all.

Rose's meddling puts her in danger. Alex will have to leave the simple peace he craves to claim a love he never could have imagined. Can they claim their happily ever after despite the turmoil?

Available now on Amazon

If you like Regency Romance, read

Inheriting Trouble

Book 1 in the Bequest Series

The inheritance was meant to better her life, not muddle it.

Georgia Holton, wellborn but nearly penniless, is best friends with one of the Earl of Sherton's five daughters. When she is invited to accompany her friend for two weeks of the Season, Georgia jumps at the opportunity to have a little adventure away from her small village.

The Earl of Crossley is handsome, wealthy, widowed, and jaded. He has no intention of courting any of this Season's debutantes. After all, every woman he's ever known has been dishonest, including his late wife. But when a chance encounter throws him into contact with the Sherton ladies and their lovely friend, he can't help being drawn to Georgia's beauty and endearing personality.

When confusion about Georgia's small inheritance becomes known, a sense of obligation to right a wrong, forces the earl and Georgia into close association.

But is she really different from any of the other women, or does she have an ulterior motive?

And can Georgia even consider getting close to a man from High Society, when all she wants is to return to her simple village life?

Sparks fly between these two, but it will take forgiveness and understanding on both their parts to reach a happily ever after.

Available now on Amazon

Other books by Wendy May Andrews you will enjoy:

Another American Historical, read:

Book 1 in the Orphan Train series:

Sophie

She'd happily give him her heart ... if only it wouldn't cost her the only home she's known

Sophie Brooks thought she had everything she could want in life. Friends, loved ones at the orphanage where she was raised, a job that gives her purpose, and a chance to help children every day ... what more could she need? But a chance encounter with a handsome stranger has her wondering if a life—and love—outside the orphanage might be exactly what she never knew she needed.

Renton Robert Rexford III has never wanted for anything. Until he meets Sophie. The charming, intelligent beauty draws him like no other. But, thanks to a disapproving benefactor who threatens to pull the orphanage's funding, his pursuit of her could cost Sophie everything she holds dear. She's all he wants in the world, but how can he ask her to give up so much when all she'd get in return is his heart?

It's not long before Sophie is forced to weigh her loyalty to the only home she's ever known against the needs of her heart. Can love prevail—or is the cost simply too high?

Available now on Amazon

Printed in Dunstable, United Kingdom

80634329R00129